T.A. Maxwell

On the Road to Big Blackfoot

On the Road to Big Blackfoot

Printed in the United States of America
First Printing, 2013
ISBN 0-9890182-8-9

Published by Zen Dog Publishing, U.S.A.

ta.maxwell@live.com
www.amazon.com/author/tamaxwell

For all of my brothers and sisters

On the Road to Big Blackfoot

"Life is like the river, sometimes it sweeps you gently along and sometimes the rapids come out of nowhere."

- Emma Smith

"I need to go to Flagstaff." I say to my friend and roommate Bear as I hit the end call button on my cellphone. We were enjoying a relaxing Thursday afternoon lounging around the house, eating unhealthy cereal, smoking a little weed, and watching a Man vs. Food marathon on the Travel Channel when I got a call from my father.

"Oh yeah. When?" Bear asks.

"Like tomorrow."

"Oh yeah. Why is that?"

"My father has cancer." Saying that seemed so surreal and I could not believe that those words had passed through my lips. I look at Bear and he looks back at me. I could tell he was searching his vocabulary bank to find the right words to respond to what I had just said.

"What kind?" This was what he had come up with.

"What do you mean?" I could not really grasp the question, even though I knew what he meant.

"What kind of cancer? Where is it?"

"Oh." I said as I shook away the imaginary cobwebs that had quickly developed in my head. "Brain cancer. That's all he said. I have brain cancer."

Bear shakes his head and comes back with "that sucks man."

"Yep, it sure does." We sit there in the living room of our three bedroom house in Venice, California, in our underwear, both shaking our heads back and forth like a couple of bobblehead dolls.

Bear and I have been roommates for two years now, but it has only been a few months that we have lived together without our other friend and roommate Max. He moved out four months ago and headed up to Seattle with his new girlfriend Caroline. They both found jobs teaching English, he, at a high school and she, at a middle school. Bear and I have become pretty close these past couple of month's but we are still different people and deal with things differently. He is more relaxed and pretty much has a whatever attitude about everything. I am more on edge and tend to freak out when things go all crazy. The weed helps but it's not the cure all.

"I need to figure out how I'm gettin' to Flag."

"Plane?" Bear suggests.

"Shit, a last minute flight will cost an arm and a leg, besides, it is not like he's on his death bed, I don't need to get there in a couple hours, more like a day or two. What about a bus?"

"Yeah, a bus will definitely be cheaper."

"Can you look online for schedules, ticket prices and shit while I look for my pack and start packing?"

"Of course man, you go pack and I'll find you a ride out of town."

"Thanks Bear." I stand up and head to my room to search for my pack. My mind is still racing as I repeat, in my head, the quick conversation my father and I just had not ten minutes ago.

"Hello."

"Hey Andrew. It's your father. How ya been?"

"Not too bad. You?"

"Well, that's sort of why I'm calling. I'm not doin' great."

"What's goin' on?"

"Well, it appears that I have brain cancer son."

"What?"

"I have brain cancer. Can you come see me? I need to see you. We need to talk."

"Yeah, I'll get there as soon as I can."

"No rush, but in the next day or two would be great."

"Okay dad, I'll see ya."

"Bye son."

Finding my pack has turned out to be a lot more difficult than I had imagined. The only place it could be is in my closet, but after throwing everything out and onto my bed, it's nowhere to be seen.

"Hey Bear, have you seen my pack?" I yell out.

"Nope, I haven't seen it since we did that weekend Yosemite hike with Max before he took off to Seattle."

"Well shit." I say so only I can hear it.

"Oh hey, I bet it's in Max's old room. Remember we put a bunch of shit in there after he left?" Bear yells back.

I smile, knowing that he is right and that is exactly where it is. The memory of throwing it in there returns as quick as it left. I exit my room and head towards Max's old room. "I bet you're right." I yell to Bear as I make my way down the hall.

"I bet I am too."

I walk in, search around for a few seconds and find it hiding in a corner of the room under a poster of the late great Johnny Cash. I grab it and head to the living room.

"You were right my brotha. The man in black was keepin' it safe."

"What?"

"Nothin'. So what's the damage on the bus fare?"

"L.A. to Flagstaff, leaving tomorrow, looks like it's gonna be eighty-five bucks."

"That's not too bad."

"Not at all. But hey I also looked on this rideshare site I go to sometimes and I found a guy who is leaving town in a couple days, headed to Colorado. He's just looking for someone to throw in for some gas. I bet you could get to Flag for forty bucks and get there faster."

"Oh yeah. But what if he's a crazy bastard or a serial killer or something?"

"Take a knife."

I laugh. "Alright email him and if he responds and takes forty I'll do it."

"Right on. It's about time for another Zen lunatic road trip." Bear says and immediately regrets. "Sorry man, I guess it's not."

"No man, it's cool, I could use a little lunacy right now."

Bear emails a message to the guy saying that I need a ride to Flagstaff to see my dying father thinking that maybe he will take me for cheaper or maybe even for free. I head back to my room and survey my clothes and pick out what I'm going to take with me. I suddenly realize that I have no idea how long I am going to be there so I pack as much as I can cram into my sixty liter pack. I decide to give the rideshare guy until the morning to reply to Bear's email. If he doesn't, then I will just head to the Greyhound bus station and buy a ticket to Flagstaff.

The next morning I wake up to the sultry sounds of Bear singing in the shower. I lay in bed for a few minutes thinking about the phone conversation I had with my father yesterday and still can't believe it. I lost my mother six years ago when I was twenty-two, after she succumbed to injuries she received after her car was t-boned by an elderly lady who had ran a red light. And now the thought of losing my other parent was thrown right in front of my face, even though the situation is a little bit different.

My parents divorced when I was eight and my mother wanted to leave Phoenix and head back to Southern California where she was born and raised. She hated Arizona, especially the heat, and she was tired of looking at nothing but the color beige or tan or sand or whatever other shades of brown there are. My father was reluctant to allow her to leave the state and take me with her, but he realized that he was the one that forced her to move to Phoenix and he felt like it was something he should do. Besides, he had ended the marriage and he figured it was the least he could do. But he did insist on being able to have me visit more often and at her expense. She agreed to let me visit two months in the summer, during my fall and spring breaks, and the week in-between Christmas and New Year's Day. As I got older though the visits decreased because I played sports and I needed to be at practice and at games during my fall and spring breaks and during parts of the summer. I usually saw him at Christmas time and a few weeks during the summer.

When I got to high school I quit playing sports but I told my father that I was still playing them so I didn't have to visit him. By this time he had moved up to Flagstaff, Arizona. It wasn't that I didn't want to see him, we just really didn't have anything in common and I was busy with school and friends and girls and I just didn't see the point.

When I turned eighteen I was not legally required to visit him anymore so I didn't. We talked on the phone now and again over the next year or so but that was pretty much it. He tried contacting me several time after that but I made no effort and I guess he just stopped trying. As I lay here, a twenty-eight year old man, I suddenly realize that I haven't seen my father in ten years and I have no idea who he is or what he might look like.

I notice the singing and the shower has stopped as I slowly rise out of bed. At that moment Bear throws open my bedroom door. He is wearing nothing but a towel...on his head.

"Hey Drewski guess what?"

"Jesus man, put some pants on."

"I will in a sec, guess what?"

"What?"

"Rideshare guy messaged me back."

"No shit. What did he say?"

"He said he's leaving tomorrow morning and he can definitely give you a ride to Flagstaff for fifty bucks."

"Fifty huh? I guess that's better than eighty-five."

"Yeah and you don't have to stop to drop off and pick up people every twenty miles."

"Alright, email him back and tell him it sounds good."

"Cool." Bear turns and starts to walk down the hall.

"Oh and give him my number so we can talk and work out the details." I yell.

"You got it buddy" he yells back as he walks down the hall to his room to hopefully put some pants on.

I give my father a quick call to tell him that I will be there tomorrow but there is no answer so I leave a message on his answering machine. Then I grab my towel and head to the bathroom to shower. I don't sing as the hot shower water pelts my body. I try to remember the last time I saw my father, what he looked like, what we talked about, and what we did.

I remember that it was the day after Christmas and that I stayed with him until New Year's Eve morning because I had big plans that night with some buddies of mine. I remember that it had snowed a few days before I had arrived. The roads were clear but most of the town, the trees, and the mountains were covered with snow. I hated snow and cold weather, which was another reason I didn't visit that much or not at all after that winter. My father was forty-seven years old at the time. I know this because I was seventeen and he was almost exactly thirty years older than me. We were both born in the month of June.

I remember he was young looking for his age and hardly had any grey in his hair or wrinkles on his face. He was taller than me by a good half foot and still probably is. I apparently got my height from my mother's side of the family. I cannot remember what we talked about or what we did but I do remember an argument we had. He wanted to take me snowboarding at the Arizona Snow Bowl and I refused. Like I said, I hated the snow and the cold and even though it was snowboarding and that I'm sure I would have had a blast I was just over it, over everything that had to do with that place, and over him. As I think back, as the bathroom turns into a steam room, I realize that I refused to do a lot of things with my father, things that any son would have loved to do, things like fishing, hiking, kayaking, and even geocaching, which is like a nature treasure hunt. I suddenly realize that I had so much animosity towards my father for divorcing my mother that I missed out on a lot of good, fun times with him and I was instantly pissed off at myself.

I turn the shower off and throw open the shower curtain. I grab the towel that I had hung over the shower curtain rod right before I entered the shower and begin to dry off my face and hair. The bathroom is filled with so much steam it's hard to see and even breathe. I almost trip on the toilet as I step out of the shower and onto the rug on the floor. At that moment Bear opens the door, letting in a rush of cold air that hits me like an avalanche.

"What the fuck man!" I yell as I try to cover my naked body with my towel to block the cold and Bear's eyes from my private business.

"What? Just wanted to let you know that rideshare guy called your cell phone and left a message."

"Thanks man but that could have waited til I got out of the shower."

"You are out of the shower."

"The bathroom then, you know what I mean."

"Yeah, yeah." Bear says as he closes the door. The bathroom is instantly warmer and I finish drying off. I head to my room, put on some clothes, and then grab my cellphone, which is charging in the living room. I call the rideshare guy, whose name is Bill, and I learn that he's a thirty-seven year old single white guy who is on his way to Colorado to camp and kayak. We agree on the fifty dollar fee for the ride to Flagstaff and he agrees to pick me up at our place at eight tomorrow morning.

When I hang up with Bill I head back to my bedroom to finish packing and make sure I have everything I need. Then I head to the living room to hang out with Bear. We decided to invite some friends over to drink some beer and wine and hopefully get a good game of dirty Jenga going, which happens several times. It is a good send off and I hit the sack around one in the morning and set the alarm for six hours later.

The alarm sounds and I hit the snooze button not once but twice. When it sounds that super annoying sound for the third time I lean over and turn it off and finally crawl out of bed, still slightly intoxicated. I quickly head to the kitchen and start a pot of coffee and then head to the bathroom to grab a couple ibuprofen tablets for my aching head. I head back to the kitchen and fill a glass with filtered water from the pitcher in the refrigerator. I toss the two pills into my mouth and then drink the entire glass of water to make sure they go down and dissolve as quickly as possible. The coffee is still not done so I decided to take a quick shower to wake up. After showering I get dressed and then head back to the kitchen to load up on caffeine. As it gets closer to eight I check my pack and make sure I have everything I need, which I do. Then I have a seat on the living room couch and sip my third cup of coffee and wait.

When the clock hits eight I decide to grab my pack and head outside to wait for my ride. I contemplate waking Bear up and saying goodbye but decide not to because he won't remember anyway. As I open the front door I notice a four door black truck pull up right in front of our place, perfect timing on both our parts. I wave and Bill waves and then exits the truck and walks towards me.

"Hey Bill." I extend my right hand.

"Hey Drew, nice to meet you." He extends his right hand and we shake. "I made some room behind the passenger seat for your bag." He says as he walks over to the right side of his truck and I follow.

"I appreciate it."

Bill opens the rear passenger door, takes my pack from me, sets it on the back seat, and then shuts the door. "You ready to hit the road?"

"Yes sir." I say as I reach into my front pants pocket, grab the fifty dollars from my money clip, and hand it to him.

"Oh. Yeah. Thanks." He says as he takes the money and shoves it into his front right pants pocket, not bothering to count it. We head to our respective doors, open them, and climb in. Bill starts up the truck and we take off down the road. We jump on Interstate 10 and head east through Los Angeles.

"So what's in Colorado if you don't mind me asking?" I ask as I look out the passenger side window at the crowded city as the sun rises.

"Lakes."

I turn my head and look at him, "Lakes?"

"Yep, lakes. I'm headed to Colorado to kayak several lakes. Nighthorse, Electra, Crystal, Ridgeway, Blue Mesa, and a couple others."

"I guess that explains the kayak attached to the roof of your truck."

"Yep. I've been planning this trip for over a year."

"Why Colorado?"

"Well I love kayaking lakes surrounded by mountains, it's insanely beautiful. And I have family in Boulder that I'm going to visit when I'm done."

"Wow, sounds like a great trip."

"Yeah it should be pretty amazing."

We merge onto the 210 freeway and continue east towards Pasadena. Bill continues to tell me about his trip and then he starts talking about his life. He tells me he was born in Denver, Colorado and spent most of his childhood there. After middle school his family moved to Boulder, a town just northwest of Denver, when his father was transferred there by his work.

After high school he moved to Northern California and attended UC Berkeley. He graduated five years later and took a job at a software company in Southern California, where he has been working and living ever since. He never married but was engaged once and has no children. He is currently single and not in any hurry to meet someone. He hates his job and wants to become a writer, which he might do, sooner than later.

We jump on Interstate 15 and head north towards Barstow. I can tell he wants to ask me about my father, but doesn't know how. I wait patiently for it, because I know it's coming, and it does sooner than later.

"So what's the status on your father if you don't mind me asking?" He finally says, reluctantly.

"All I know is that he has brain cancer. Not sure how bad it is or how long he's had it. He called me a couple days ago, told me he had it, asked me to come see him, so here I am."

"Brain cancer. Shit man I'm sorry. That sucks."

"Yeah it does."

"Are you guys close?"

"I haven't seen him in ten years. Shit, that was the first time I had talked with him in eight years now that I think about it."

"I take it your parents aren't together anymore?"

"Nope. Divorced when I was eight. My mother passed away six years ago."

"Damn, I'm sorry man."

"Shit happens. We have no control over any of it. When we're supposed to go, we go."

"That's true."

We reach Barstow and after stopping for a restroom break and grabbing a drink at a roadside gas station we merge onto Interstate 40 and head east towards the California/Arizona border. Flagstaff is only five hours away. As we leave Barstow behind, Bill starts up a new conversation, even though I would rather not, but I don't want to be rude.

"So what line of work are you in Drew?"

"Retail." Bill doesn't respond and I get the feeling that my short response offended him so I elaborate. "I work at a grocery store."

"Oh yeah. You like it?"

"It's okay. It pays the bills."

"No college?" I don't respond quickly enough. "I apologize. That was out of line. I didn't mean that to imply anything."

"Nah it's cool. I started college but my mother passed away during my junior year and I just never finished. I do pretty well though at my job, money is decent, and it's low stress, so it's all good."

"Well, I am a perfect example of a college degree not meaning a damn thing."

"What do you mean?"

"Well like I told you earlier I hate being a software engineer and I'm about to give it up. That's what this trip is really about. It's my vision quest, my spiritual walkabout. I want to travel and write, which makes my degree garbage."

"That's awesome man, good for you." I smile because Bill reminds me of Max, who always talks about taking vision quests and going on spiritual walkabouts, but then I start to feel sad because I miss that damn Zen lunatic. "So what happened? What made you decide to become a writer?" I say to distract me from my sad thoughts.

"I had an epiphany one day. I was in a lousy relationship. I wasn't happy at work. I didn't have any real friends. And I didn't have the relationship I wanted to have with my family." I look at Bill and I can see tears welling up in his eyes. "So I started to reevaluate my life and tried to figure out what was important and what I needed to do to be happy. I eventually came up with a mantra I guess you can say. Three things that I needed to do to be happy."

"And those are?"

"To be happy I believe people need to love three things. One, you have to love yourself, inside and out. Two, you have to love other people, your friends, your family, your significant other, etcetera. And finally, you have to love what you do, for work and for pleasure."

I think about what Bill just said for a few seconds. "I like that man and I agree with it completely."

"It's a lot of hard work to change those things, but I think it's what we have to do to be happy. I mean how can you not be happy if you love yourself, other people, and your job?"

"Man there is no way you wouldn't be happy if you had all that love flowing through you." I add.

As we drive over the Colorado River and enter Arizona the conversation has ceased and what Bill said a short while ago about love is bouncing around in my head. Do I love myself? I think so. I mean I'm in decent shape and I'm not a bad looking guy. I also like my personality. I don't think I annoy people and I believe I'm a good friend. Do I love what I do? Well I wouldn't say I love my job but it's fulfilling and I don't really have any complaints. And when it comes to pleasure I love writing poetry, and partying, and hiking, and just being a Zen lunatic. Do I love other people? Well I love my friends. I don't have a wife or a girlfriend so I guess that's something to work on. When it comes to family I love my father, but not as much as I should. Maybe this trip is my opportunity to work on my relationship with him. As I think about him I decide that I should probably give him a call and let him know that I'm close.

An hour and a half later we enter the Flagstaff city limits and I tell Bill to take exit 195 and head north into the heart of Flagstaff. Not far from Interstate 40 on Milton Road is a Denny's where I'm meeting my father. As we enter the parking lot I see my father standing in front of the place by the front door. Bill stops and I jump out. I grab my pack, thank Bill for the ride, and shut the door.

I walk up to my father who I hardly recognize. He looks forty years older than when I saw him last. He is thin and what little hair he has is white as snow. He is wearing jeans and a flannel shirt. Under that he is wearing a black t-shirt that says

"FUCK CANCER" in large white letters on the front of it, which makes me smile. He is also sporting a pair of brown Birkenstock sandals, with socks, which I hate, and of course his signature black rimmed glasses.

"Father."

"Son. How was the ride?"

"Good."

"Good. Hungry?"

"Starving." I say as we head inside.

CHAPTER TWO

We stand in front of the register waiting on a hostess to seat us, which happens after a couple of minutes. We take a seat in a small booth, my father on one side, me on the other. The hostess sets down two menus on the table and tells us that our server will be with us shortly. A few seconds later a young women, probably in her mid-twenties, with long brown hair put up in a quick ponytail approaches our table. She is a curvy gal and has a very pretty face. She smiles, which makes her even more attractive.

"How ya'll doin' today?" she asks in a southern accent, which catches me off guard. "Can I start ya'll off with some drinks?" She is still smiling and I notice her big green eyes as

I answer.

"Coffee for me."

"Decaf please." My father adds.

"Okay, a regular and a decaf. I'll grab those real quick and be right back to take ya'lls order." She walks off, still smiling. I turn my head and watch her walk away.

"That's some Georgia peach." My father says.

I turn my head back towards him. "Sure is." I say with a smile, which I lose almost instantly when I realize why I am there. "So…how've you been, considering."

"Not too bad son, not too bad. I have good days and bad day and day's in-between." He says with a half-smile.

Our server returns with the two coffees and a tin container of creamer and sets them on the table. I make an effort to locate her name tag so I can call her by name. That's something I make a habit of doing. I think it's nice and just polite to call someone that is serving you by their name. Plus it might make the service better, which means I have to tip more, but it's worth it. They don't make a decent hourly wage anyway and I like a reason to tip more.

"You gentlemen know what ya'll want or do ya need a couple of minutes?"

That smile is killing me. I look up at her with huge smile of my own. "You know Raelynn, we haven't even looked at our menus yet, could you be a doll and give us a few minutes." She is taken back, either because I called her by her name or because I called her doll, I'm not sure.

"Of course sweetie. I'll be back in a few." She says with that hypnotic smile still frozen on her pretty face. She walks off and I notice my father watching her walk away this time.

"Those damn Georgia peaches. They get ya every time." He says and I smile and nod my head in agreement. I grab my menu and so does he. I quickly skim through it for no real reason since I already know what I want. I basically get the same thing every time I go to a place like this. My father on the other hand, from what I remember, takes forever. He examines everything on the menu. I remember one time when I was a kid he literally took a half an hour to order, he read every description for every item in the damn thing. By the time he was finished I thought I was going to starve to death and he just ended up ordering a damn cheeseburger. Well apparently he's changed his ways because he set the menu down seconds after I did.

"You know what you want already?" I said in a surprised tone. He responded with a small chuckle.

"I'm not as anal as I used to be son. Getting the cancer gives you a different perspective on life and I don't have the time to spend half a day perusing the menu like I used to." He called it "the cancer" like it was this big important thing like the President or something, but it was big and it was important and it was then that I realized all of this was real and that I needed to know more about what was going on.

Raelynn reappeared out of nowhere, pad and pen in hand. "You gentlemen ready to order." She says, smiling like always. I nod towards my father for him to go first.

"I will have the spinach scramble with egg whites, a side of hash browns, and an order of sourdough toast, extra toasted please."

"And for you sweetie?" She says with her big green eyes staring down at me.

"I will have an order of hotcakes with a side of bacon and an English muffin." I grab both of the menus as she finishes writing our order in her pad. When she's done I hand her the menus, which she grabs. Our eyes lock and we smile at each other.

"Thank you." I say.

"Of course sweetie. I will have it out to you gentlemen in two shakes of a lamb's tail." She walks off and I look back again to watch her walk away, except this time she turns her head around and catches me. I quickly turn back towards my father and he just smiles and says "busted."

I shrug my shoulders and smile and begin to prepare my coffee for consumption; a two second pour of creamer and four packets of real sugar. That fake shit is for the birds. My father takes a drink of his decaf. He drinks his coffee black. I think that's when you know you're old, when you drink your coffee black.

"So how've ya been son?"

"I've been good. Just been workin' and livin' life."

"That's great. I'm happy that you're doing well." He takes another sip of his coffee. I nod my head and follow his lead.

We sit there for the next minute or so drinking coffee and looking in all different sorts of directions occasionally making eye contact with one another. It was an awkward moment and I could tell he was thinking the same thing. Luckily Raelynn walked up to refill our coffees, which broke the silence.

"Food should be out soon gentlemen." She said with that beautiful southern accent and smile.

"Thank you Raelynn. We appreciate it." I say with a smile of my own. She walks away but I don't look back, fearful that she will catch me looking at her again. I notice my father smile and then laugh a little bit.

"What?" He continues to smile. "What are you smiling at old man?"

He laughs again. "She turned to see if you were looking at her again. I think she likes you." He continues to smile and it makes me smile, not because she might possibly like me, which wouldn't be a bad thing, but because he is smiling and even though it has been ten years since I 've seen him and even though we have never really gotten along, I like seeing him happy, especially now.

Raelynn returns with our food right as my father is about to say something. She sets our food down in front of us and asks if we need anything else. I tell her we are fine and she walks off again, smiling of course. I begin to prepare my hotcakes for consumption by spreading a little butter and then a lot of maple syrup on them. My father grabs the tabasco sauce, twists off the cap, and starts to stab his spinach egg white scrabble with it, at least that is what it looks like. It is a bitch getting tabasco sauce out of that bottle. As we begin to eat my father chimes in.

"So, I have some news."

"Oh yeah, and what's that?"

"I didn't ask you to come up here just to talk."

I am about to take a drink of my coffee, but lower it right before it reaches my lips, and then I set it back down. "Okay." I wait for him to continue.

"I need you to come up to the Big Blackfoot with me?"

"The Big Blackfoot?" I say, not knowing what or where that is.

"It's a river up in Montana?" My eyes grow wide.

"You need me to go to a river with you? In Montana?"

"Yes."

"Dad, I can't go with you to Montana. I have work. I have bills to pay. I have shit to do." He takes a bite of his spinach scramble and then wipes his mouth.

"I need you there son."

"Why? What's so important that you need me to travel a thousand miles up to some river in Montana with you?"

"Cause I want you to be my best man." The words linger in my head and I try to absorb what he just said.

"Your best man?" And then it hits me. "You're getting married?"

"I am."

I'm in shock, but then I realize that I haven't talked

to him in eight years and a lot can happen in that amount of time. "In Montana? You're getting married in Montana?"

"Yes, a week from today."

I'm totally blown away by this news so I take a couple of bites from my stack of pancakes and mull over this new information. "I have so many questions. I don't even know where to begin."

"Well, why don't we finish eating, you can think about it, and then we can head back to the house and I'll answer all of your questions then, okay?"

"Yeah, I guess." He takes another bite of his spinach scramble and I take a drink of my coffee as questions begin to form in my mind.

"And how are you fine young gentlemen doin'? How's the food?" Raelynn appears out of nowhere. I can't answer her as I am preoccupied at the moment so my father takes the reigns.

"We're doing great Raelynn and the food is fantastic. Would you be a doll and get the check for us?"

"Leavin' so soon?" She is sincerely sad.

"Yeah, we have some things we have to get done around the house."

"Well, that's no fun. Let me go grab that check for ya. I'll be right back."

My father smiles. "Thank you dear."

She looks at me but the smile from before is not there. I smile at her and a second later there it is, that big beautiful smile. She walks away and I go back to my mental question formation. My father finishes up his cup of decaf and Raelynn returns with the check.

"You two have a great day and make sure to come back and see me soon." She smiles at me and winks.

"You have a great rest of your day too Raelynn and I'm sure we'll see you again. My names Drew by the way and this is my father John."

"It's nice to meet you Drew and you too John."

"It's been our pleasure Raelynn." My father says.
With that she smiles and then walks off. I look back at her and she turns her head and smiles.

"Busted again." My dad says as I turn my head back towards him. All I can do is smile and continue to wonder why the hell my father is get married and why the hell it's happening up in Montana. "You ready?"

"Yeah." I say as I take a final sip of coffee.

We get up, pay the bill at the front register, and then head to my dad's truck, a blue 1994 Chevy Silverado Z71, complete with a low profile snap-on truck bed cover.

As we drive to my dad's house I look out the passenger side window still thinking about all the things my father has said to me these past couple of days, the cancer and now a wedding. My head is a mixed jumble on thoughts and questions. The roads outside are clear but there are small mounds of snow on the sides of the road like a snow plow had scraped it over there a few days ago. The snow is melting and heavily spotted with dirt and debris taking away from its natural beauty. But even though there is snow on the sides of the streets the people outside are wearing light jackets or flannel shirts. I turn and look at my father.

"What's up with the snow?"

"We had a late storm roll in a few days ago and cover us in a nice little blanket of snow."

"Wow, it's almost May"

"Yeah it happens, but as you can see the temperature has gone up and we're finally in full spring mode." Yeah the temperature has gone up, but it's still only sixty degrees and the flannel shirt I have on isn't doing a thing for me. My father notices that I'm cold, probably because I'm hugging myself. "I have a coat you can have when we get to the house Mr. California." He smiles.

I chuckle. "Thanks…and you do know that is snows in California? A lot actually."

"Of course I do, but I'm gonna assume you don't live in those parts. That is unless you moved since we talked last."

"No, I'm still in L.A., Venice to be exact."

We finally get to my dad's place and I notice the FOR SALE sign right away.

"You're selling the house?"

"Let's get inside and we'll talk all about it over a couple of beers."

"Okay…wait, you can drink beer? I thought you couldn't drink?"

He stops the truck, turns the ignition off, and looks at me.

"Why cause I have cancer?" I nod my head. "Shit son, I'm not gonna let a little thing like brain cancer stop me front enjoying an ice cold beer." At that, I think to myself, man he's changed a lot since the last time I saw him. Then I remember, that was ten years ago and people change, I know I have.

"Okay." I say as I shrug my shoulders and then we exit the truck. I grab my pack and we head inside.

I head to my room and toss my pack on the floor next to the bed. It looks nothing like it did ten years ago. There is just a bed and a half dozen taped up boxes along the far wall. I head to the living room and my father is throwing a few logs into the fireplace. There are more taped up boxes littering the living room. He hears me enter.

"Can you grab us a couple beers from the fridge?"

"Sure thing." I walk into the kitchen, which is also littered with taped up boxes, except for one that is still open. I open the refrigerator and search for the beers.

"There are a couple glasses in the cabinet next to the fridge that I haven't packed yet." He yells from the living room.

"Okay." I finally find his collection of beers on the lower shelf and grab two. They are cans of Lumberyard IPA, from a local brewery. I set them on the counter and then grab two pint glasses from the cabinet. I pop the tops of the beers and pour them into the glasses. I head back to the living room just as my father gets the fire going. He stands up, turns towards me, and I hand him one of the beers.

"Thank you son." He says as he takes the glass and takes a

drink. I follow his lead and do the same. "Have a seat, let's talk." He points to one of the two big brown leather chairs that are hugging the fireplace.

"Okay." I walk over and take a seat, in what might just be the most comfortable chair I have ever sat in. He sits in the other chair and we sit there for a few minutes looking at the fire, watching it and listening to it crackle, enjoying our Lumberyard IPAs. I decide to break the silence. "I don't remember these chairs, are they new?"

"Well not really, I got them a few years ago, so they're not new to me, but to you I guess they are."

"Yeah, I wanted to talk to you about that dad. I'm really sorry…"

He cuts me off. "Son, I get it. Don't worry about it, the past is the past, I'm sorry, you're sorry, let's just sweep it under the rug and focus on the now and the future."

"Okay, but I need to say one thing."

"Alright, go ahead, one thing."

I take a deep breath and exhale. "I blamed you for the divorce and I never gave you a chance. It was all me. You tried, but I just couldn't get over it and I'm sorry."

He cracks a little side smile. "I could have tried harder son. It's not all on you. And the divorce was my fault. You were right to be upset, but if you look how it turned out, it was the right thing. Your mother was way happier in the long run and honestly so was I. Everything happens for a reason son." We take another drink of our beers. "So, I'm sure you have a ton of questions bouncing around in that head of yours, so go ahead and ask away when you're ready."

The fire crackles and I look at it. I stare at the glowing red and orange embers and it puts me in a trance. The heat from it warms my entire body and I remember sitting in front of it as a kid, staring at it in the same way. A loud crackle breaks my trance and I look back at my father, who is staring at the fire too. He looks so much older than he did ten years ago. He takes another drink from his glass and looks back at me.

"Tell me about the cancer and I want you to be brutally honest with me, no bullshit." I say staring right back at him.

"Okay. I have stage four brain cancer and there's no stopping it. I only have a month, maybe two." His words pierce my heart like a knife and tears well up in my eyes. "They found it a couple months ago when I went in to see my doctor after weeks of really intense headaches, which I thought were just migraines." The tears begin to slide down my cheeks.

"You've known for two months and you're telling me now?" My voice slightly raised.

"I didn't know how to tell you and I guess I just couldn't believe it myself. I didn't want to believe it. I thought there is no way that could happen to me. But when I saw another doctor a month ago, just to get a second opinion, he confirmed it."

"So chemo can't stop it? Radiation? Medications? Nothing?"

He shakes his head. "It's too far along. There's nothing that can be done."

At that moment, every negative feeling I have ever had about my father quickly vacates my body and I hate myself for wasting the past ten plus years on childhood animosity. I felt so helpless, that I couldn't do anything to stop this from happening. And right then, I decide to make the most of the time I have left with my father. I don't even know this man and I pledge to myself to get to know him.

"This is unbelievable." I look back at the crackling fire. "I can't believe this is happening."

"I know the feeling son, but it is happening, which is why I finally did call you and why I asked you to come here."

His words remind me about the wedding and I change the subject to that as I look back at him. "So what's the deal with this wedding?" I wipe the tears from my face with the sleeve of my flannel shirt. I finish my beer as my father finishes his.

"Let me go grab us a couple fresh beers before we can get into that." He stands up, takes my glass, and heads to the kitchen. As he grabs the beers, I stare at the fire again trying to absorb this new information, trying to make sense of it all. He returns and hands me a fresh pint of Lumberyard IPA, which I take from him. He sits back down and looks at the fire as he takes a drink.

"So, the wedding?" I ask again.

He looks at me. "Yes, the wedding. Well I guess I should start from the beginning." He takes another drink of his IPA.

"Well for the past eight years or so I've spent my summers traveling up to Montana to fly fish the Big Blackfoot River."

My eyes get wide. "Really? I never knew you were into fishing."

"I wasn't which is why I was confused when you gave me a book about it for my birthday one year."

"I did?"

"You don't remember?"

I try to but there is nothing. "Not at all."

"I think it was when you were in high school, not too long before you graduated."

"What was the book?"

"*A River Runs Through it*."

The memory comes back to me in a flash. "Yeah, I remember now. I was a senior and mom was getting on me about sending you something for your birthday. We were at a bookstore so I just grabbed the first book I saw, which was that one."

He smiles. "Well it took me a couple years to actually pick it up and read it, but when I did it hit me. It was a great book and then I found out that it was made into a movie and I watched it and I said to myself that's it, I'm gonna go up to Montana and fly fish the Big Blackfoot."

I have a stunned look on my face. "So you just went up there and started fly fishin' it?"

"Yeah, pretty much. I packed a bag, hopped in the truck, and drove up to Missoula. When I got there I found a cheap motel room, bought a rod and some flies, and just went for it."

"Did you catch anything?"

He starts laughing. "Hell no, you can't just grab a rod and go fly fish, there's a lot more to it than that, which I realized real quick. Hell, I couldn't even cast the damn thing."

I shake my head and laugh with him. The cancer thing is buried, for now. "So what did you do?"

"Well I brought the DVD with me and watched it again in the motel room. I fast forwarded to the fly fishing scenes and tried to learn that way."

"Did it work?"

"Hell no. I went out the next day and tried again and it was an utter disaster, but…" He pauses and takes a drink of his beer and I do the same. The fire continues to crackle in the background. "There was this other fisherman close by and he came over and offered to help me if I needed it, which I absolutely did. I met him the next day and the day after and we became good friends. I meet up with him every time I go up."

"That's cool."

"Yeah, he taught me how to fly fish that summer and for free none the less, well if you don't count the hundreds of beers I've bought him over the past eight years."

"You're not marrying him are you?"

He laughs. "No son, I'm getting to that be patient."

"I know dad I was just messing with you." Of course I didn't know, maybe he did go gay. It wasn't like I knew who he was.

He continues. "So two summers ago when I was up there Jim, that's his name, and I were at our usual drinking spot enjoying a few beers when I noticed this gal over at the jukebox flipping through the song catalog. Well, I actually noticed her ass first since her back was to us." I laugh and he smiles. "When she turned around I was blown away. You know that feeling when you first see someone and you instantly see your future together?" I nod my head even though I had never experienced that. "It was that kind of feeling. Now I have never been a believer of love at first sight, but that was basically what happened." He smiles as he remembers that moment. "She had dark brown wavy hair, which fell just below her shoulder blades. And her body, man was her body amazing, not too skinny, not too thick, it was perfect and I just stared at her until she sat back down with two other women. I told Jim that I wasn't leaving until I talked to her." He pauses and I notice the spark in my father's eyes as he stares off in the distance and remembers it. I can tell at that moment that even though he has cancer, he is happier now than he has ever been.

"So did you talk to her?"

He snaps out of it. "I did. I told the waitress that I wanted to buy them their next round and when the waitress told them, they all looked over and smiled. When they got their drinks they waved us over and we got up, walked over, and sat with them. We talked for hours and it was the easiest conversation I had ever had with a woman." He pauses again as he remembers it. He takes a drink of his IPA and I do the same.

"So you got her number I assume?"

He snaps out of it again. "I did. I called her the next day and we met for dinner and the rest, as they say, is history."

"So what's her name by the way?"

He laughs. "Sorry, I forget that you don't know any of this. Her name is Sarah."

"Well I can't wait to meet her dad."

"I can't wait for you to meet her either son." He takes another drink. "Oh and I just realized something."

"What's that?"

"She has a daughter, so I guess you're gonna have a new sister."

I perk up. "Really?"

"Yep."

"And what's her name?"

"Her name is Jessica. She's twenty-five and lives in Missoula, not too far from us."

"Us?"

"Yeah, I guess I haven't mentioned that yet either. I moved up to Missoula a few months ago with her, which is why the house is for sale. I actually haven't been down here since then."

"No shit."

"No shit." He echoes.

"So I take it the wedding is happening because of the

cancer?"

"Yep, when we found out about the cancer she told me the next day that she wanted to marry me and I told her that there would be nothing that would make me happier. She has been planning it ever since. She's actually the one that pushed me to contact you after she asked me who my best man was going to be. At first I told her it would be Jim, but the more I thought about it, the more I realized that this was an opportunity for us to reconnect and after that it was a no brainer. So I called you and here we are."

"Well I'm honored dad, even though I wasn't your first choice." I smile and he shakes his head.

"You were always my first choice deep down son." I smile. We finish our second beers. "So, are you hungry again?"

"I could eat."

"Okay well why don't ya go unpack and I will order us a pizza."

"Okay. I think I'm gonna jump in the shower real quick if that's cool?"

"Yeah, of course, I left a towel in the hall bathroom for ya."

"Okay, thanks." We get up and I head to my bedroom as my father grabs his phone and orders our dinner.

I finish showering and get dressed just as the doorbell rings. I head to the kitchen where my father is getting paper plates for the pizza that is sitting on the counter. He opens the pizza box and the smell of cheese and pepperoni punches me in the nose. My stomach grumbles saying feed me that awesomeness right now. I grab a slice and set it on my paper plate and my father does the same. We eat our first slices without saying a word, enjoying every delicious bite. We both grab a second slice and I break the silence.

"So what's up with the house? Is it sold?"

"It is. The movers are coming in the morning."

"So are we headed up to Missoula tomorrow then?" I say with a mouthful of pizza.

"Yeah, if you wanna go."

"Of course I wanna go. It will be a fun little father and son Zen lunatic road trip."

"A Zen what?" He says, confused.

Nothing dad, it's just what my buddies and I call ourselves."

"Oh, okay." He takes a bite of pizza. "Damn, I just realized that I haven't given you a chance to talk about what is goin' on with you. So what's goin' on with you?"

"Not much really. I live in Venice with my roommate and I work at a grocery store, that's about it."

"No girlfriend?"

"Nope."

"Hmm, any prospects?"

"Not really, I was dating this chick I work with, but that didn't work out, then she transferred to another store up near San Francisco."

The conversation stalls as there's not much to my boring

life, except for my trips into the mountains of California, which I'm not in the mood to talk about. When we finish our pizza we head back to the comfy chairs by the fire with fresh IPAs and just sit there, in silence and relax. Then my father shocks me with a question.

"So, you wanna smoke some weed?" I look at him like did you really just ask me that question?

"Are you serious?"

"Yeah, my doctor put me on it. It's good stuff, helps with the pain and insomnia." I'm still in shock but shrug it off.

"Yeah, okay."

"Let me grab my bong, I'll be right back."

He gets up and leaves the room and I'm just like did my father just say let me grab my bong? And I laugh and shake my head. I think to myself who is this guy? While my father is out of the room I decide to give my boss Joe a call and let him know what is going on. He tells me not to worry about it and to just call him again when I get back home. I thank him for being cool and we hang up. I also give Bear a call and update him on what's going on.

My father walks back into the living room with a small clear plastic bong in his right hand and he sits back down. He packs it, lights it, and takes a hit. He passes the bong and the lighter over to me and exhales the smoke. "I have to use a bong. Smoking out of a pipe or from a joint burns too much."

I nod my head, light it, take a hit, and pass it back to him. This goes on for a few more minutes and he was right, it is good shit. I'm exhausted so I tell my father that I'm going to hit the sack. He says okay and I get up and head towards my bedroom. As I do, I turn my head and look towards my father, who can't see me, and I smile and then tears begin to well up in my eyes as I remember the cancer, that fucking cancer.

CHAPTER THREE

I wake up to the sound of someone gently knocking on my bedroom door.

"Yeah." I answer.

"Movers are here." My father says through the door.

"Okay." I rub my eyes and stretch my arms and legs out.

"I ran down and got us some coffee and donuts. It's in the kitchen."

"Okay, I'll be there in a sec." I look over at the digital clock that is still on the night stand and it reads eight fifteen. I haven't been up this early two days in a row in a long time and my body feels it. After a few more minutes in bed I finally throw the covers off of me and jump out of bed. I put on the pants I wore the day before and then throw on a nice clean flannel shirt over the white V-neck I slept in. When I open the bedroom door I almost trip over a pair of slippers that my father had apparently left for me and thank God because the floor is freezing. I slide my feet into the slippers that are about two sizes too small but they work and I head to kitchen.

When I get to the kitchen the two moving guys are in the living room talking with my father. I grab one of the coffees and take a sip. My father walks over. "Morning son." He grabs the other coffee.

"Morning father. Thanks for the coffee." I take another sip.

"No problem, don't forget to grab a donut or two or three." He points at the pink donut box on the other counter.

"Oh I won't, I have a very passionate relationship with donuts." I smile and he laughs.

"Yeah, so do I." He says rubbing his belly, which is as flat as it can be, and I laugh. His appetite seems to be in good shape, which is probably attributed to the marijuana. I can only imagine if he had to go through chemo what shape his body would be in. He had always been a thin guy, mainly because he ran and ate a healthy diet most of his adult life. I remember when I used to visit him how I hated eating the food that he made, but I choked it down, just so I could have pizza the next day. That's what he would do, he would make a healthy meal for us and if I ate it he would order a pizza the next night. Then the night after that he would make another healthy meal and so on. I guess he just figured that three or four healthy meals a week was better than none.

"So what's the plan?" I ask as the memory fades away and I make my way over to the donut box.

"Well, they should have everything packed up in an hour or so and then we can take off."

I grab a maple long john from the box and take a bite. "Yeah I noticed you don't have that much stuff here anymore."

He walks over and grabs a powdered jelly donut from the box and takes a bite. "Yeah, just before I went up to Missoula to live with Sarah I had a huge yard sale and sold a ton of stuff. I also took some stuff up with me that she didn't have that we could use."

"You guys have room up there for all this stuff?"

"Not really, which is why most of it is going into storage. I'll probably just end up selling most of it after the wedding. We told people not to buy us any wedding gifts, just to come and be a part of it. We don't need any more shit." We both laugh.

"So where are we headed today? Moab?" I take a drink of my coffee and my father takes a drink of his.

"Well, I was thinking we would go another way."

"Okay and which way is that?"

He smiles at me. "Through Vegas." I shake my head and smile. "Well I figured that since you're the best man and all you'd want to throw me a bachelor party and what better place than Vegas. Besides, one last Vegas trip before I die is seriously needed." That's the first time that he's said the word die and I don't like it one bit.

"Alright old man, Vegas it is. So where do you want to stay?"

He smiles at me again. "Caesar's."

My eyes get wide. "I work at a grocery store dad, I can't afford Caesar's."

"Just because you're the best man doesn't mean you have to pay for the bachelor party. I made a ton of money on the sale of this house and besides, I booked the room a week ago." He winks at me and I shake my head and smile again. "Now eat some more of those donuts, we'll need the energy for tonight." He leaves the kitchen and heads outside. I take another donut, an apple fritter this time, and go to town on it. When I finish it I grab another, a sour cream old fashioned, and head to my bedroom to repack the stuff that I unpacked for some reason the night before.

The moving guys finish packing up all my father's stuff in just under an hour and then take off down the road towards Missoula. They should get there about the same time we do, in three or four days. My father tells me that the plan after Vegas is to head north on highway 93, which is a straight shot up to Missoula, through Nevada and Idaho. I look at the map he has and it is definitely the most direct route, but it is definitely not the fastest way. It looks like it's a single lane highway most of the way, which is fine because we're not in that much of a hurry. We just have to get there by Thursday, which shouldn't be a problem considering its Sunday morning.

I throw our packs in the back of the truck and my dad tosses the cooler in the cab. He locks the house up and we stand there for a good minute just staring at it, basically saying goodbye to the old place. We hop in the truck and head to the realty office to drop off the keys. Then we drive through town, stopping at a gas station mini-mart to get ice, drinks, and snacks. Then we jump on Interstate 40 and head west towards Vegas.

"So what have you been up to son? Besides living in Venice, working at a grocery store, and not having a girlfriend." He starts the first of many conversations I assume we will have on this thousand mile trip up to Montana. And I instantly feel terrible about ignoring his attempts to contact me in the past and I feel I owe him an explanation.

"Well, first off I just want to say that I'm sorry dad for not calling you back when you would call after I turned eighteen, I regret that now more than I can even express and not because you are...you know, but just because."

"It's fine son, like I said last night the past is the past. It's not about what we have done, it's about what we will do. This trip isn't about a wedding, hell we could have flown to Missoula, this trip is about us reconnecting. Forget everything that happened it's over and done with. Let's just start right here right now." I look at him and I see a wise man, a man that might just be an old school Zen lunatic and I smile.

"Okay."

"Good, so what have you been up to?"

"I thought you said forget about the past?" He looks at me and I laugh. "Just messin' with ya old man. Well, after high school I took a semester off to just figure shit out and then I started up at West L.A. College, which is a small two year college in Culver City. Then after that I transferred to Long Beach State. But then mom died during my first year there and I stopped going." I pause as I think about my mother.

"I'm real sorry about your mom Andrew."

"No, I'm sorry, I should have called you and told you. I just…"

He cuts me off. "It's okay son, I found out soon after."

"How?"

"Mutual friends of ours that I still kept in contact with after the divorce called me and ask if I had heard and I said that I hadn't. I cried off and on for a good week. I loved your mother son, I did, very much so, but I changed over the last two years of our marriage and I met someone else and it was just over for us."

"You cheated on mom?"

"No, no, no, nothing happened with that woman until after I left. And I didn't leave your mother for her, I would have left regardless. I don't know marriage and relationships are complicated things, which I'm sure you know."

"Yes they are which is why I'm still single at twenty-eight." I look out the window at the Northern Arizona landscape and think about Emily, the one that got away.

"So what have you been doing since then?"

I snap out of it and look at him. "Oh working mostly."

"Yeah, you said you work at a grocery store?"

"I do."

"You like it?"

"Yeah, I mean it pays pretty well, my bosses are cool, and it's sort of easy and fun at times so…"

"You ever gonna finish college?"

"I don't know, I think about it from time to time but Long Beach is a ways away and the thought of sitting in a classroom listening to some snooty professor talking about whatever makes me wanna puke. And then there's writing papers and reading boring textbooks, God the thought just makes me cringe. And honestly dad I have no idea what I would even study anymore."

"What was your major?"

I laugh and shake my head. "Philosophy."

He looks at me and we both laugh. "Shit son, just living life is a degree in philosophy." I smile and think to myself, Yep my father is an old school Zen lunatic for sure. "So you live in Venice with a couple guys?"

"Yeah, well one other guy, there was three of us but Max moved up to Seattle with his girlfriend. Now it's just me and Bear.

"Bear?"

"Yeah, well Barry's his name but we've always called him Bear. It's short for Barry, obviously, and he's more of a Bear than a Barry anyway. He's a real crazy fucker." At that moment I wonder what Bear is up to right now. I would guess he's in the living room smoking weed in his tie-dyed robe watching Man vs. Food on the Travel Channel. I smile at the thought.

"So, you're twenty-eight, single, you work at a grocery store, and you live with a guy named Bear?" I think about it for a second and wonder if my father thinks I'm a loser.

"Yeah that's pretty much it. Not the most successful life."

He looks at me. "Do you know what the definition of success is? It's the achievement of something desired, planned, or attempted. If you're good at your job and you love it, then you're successful. That shit about success being only about money and fame is bullshit and overrated. Being happy is what's important. Are you happy son?" I think about the question for a few seconds.

"I am." I finally say.

"Then that's all that matters."

We sit there in silence for a few minutes and I soak in what my father had just said. I think about the question again, am I happy? And I am, except for one thing. "I do wish sometimes that I had someone to share my life with. I mean Bear is awesome, but a woman's company would be nice."

"It will come son, when the time is right the perfect woman will come out of nowhere and turn your world upside-down." Since Max met Caroline I've been thinking more about love and starting a family, but I've never been too good with the ladies. My father is right though, it will happen at some point; at least I hope it will.

We reach Kingman and stop for lunch at In n' Out Burger. I get the usual, a double-double animal style, which means it has grilled onions, pickles, extra spread, and mustard cooked into each patty. I also order my fries animal style, which means the fries are topped with spread, grilled onions, and cheese. The spread is basically just a version of thousand island dressing and the animal style is part of their somewhat secret menu, which is nowhere on the actual menu. You have to be from the west coast to know. Those of us born here are just implanted with this kind of information; I swear it's in our DNA from conception. My father orders the same and we sit at one of the two-seater tables and enjoy our burgers and fries.

After lunch we continue north out of Kingman on highway 93, Vegas is only a hundred miles away.

"So what about you dad, what have you been up to these past ten years?"

"Let's save that for after Vegas, it's a long story. Let's listen to some music."

"Okay." We spend the next hour listening to everything from Hall and Oates to Rush to my dad's favorite band the Eagles. We sing out loud to every song as we make our way north towards the Hoover Dam. We get to the Hoover Dam an hour later and stop to check it out, which we've done many times in the past, but my father wants to see it one last time. We ask a nice German couple if they can take our picture with the Dam behind us and they oblige. We walk across the top of the Dam, looking over the side several times.

"Did you know there are bodies frozen in the concrete of this dam from workers who fell in during the building of it?" my father asks me.

"Yes father, you tell me every time we come here."

"I do?"

"Yes."

"Oh."

I'm not even sure if he's right but I decide not to argue with him about it. I tried that once before and it ended up with us not talking all the way back to Flagstaff.

We head back to the truck and cross the dam again. We wind our way out of the canyon and pass Lake Mead, which is to our right, as we head into Boulder City. Twenty minutes later we enter the Las Vegas valley. We drive through Henderson and then reach Interstate 15 several minutes later. We head east of Interstate 15 for a short distance, exit, and reach our destination, Caesar's Palace Hotel and Casino.

We self-park because my father doesn't trust valets and my first thought is what the hell are they going to steal, his tape deck? He finds a parking spot close to the elevator, surprisingly. We grab our packs and head inside. As we make our way through the casino floor the familiar sound and lights of the slot machines stimulate our ears and eyes. I automatically want a beer and a cigarette. We reach the front desk and my father checks us in. We head to our room, which is an amazing two room suite.

"Are you serious with this room?" I ask.

"It's my last Vegas trip son, might as well do it up right." I nod my head in agreement. "Let's shower and then head down and play some blackjack."

"Sounds good to me." I say as I head to my room and toss my pack on the bed. I unpack some clothes for the night and then hop in the shower. The hot shower water feels amazing and I stand under it for a good ten minutes. When I am thoroughly relaxed I turn the water off, grab a towel, and dry off. I get dressed and head into the main room of the suite where my father is waiting on the couch.

"Damn son it's about time. I was about to make sure you didn't drowned in there."

"Sorry, the water felt too good, I could have spent another twenty minutes in there."

"Yeah I hear ya, it was nice. You ready to head down and lose some money?"

"Yep, let's rock n, roll."

He stands up and we head out the door to the elevators. We exit the elevator and are attacked by that oh so familiar sound. As we make our way to the blackjack tables I see the usual suspects on the slot machines. An old lady playing the nickel slots, smoking a cigarette, and drinking a gin and tonic. A group of women wearing ridiculous outfits, one of them wearing a tiara, an obvious bachelorette party. A wannabe high-roller in a suit playing the dollar slots, drinking a martini. And of course a doped up loser trying to win the rent money that he blew on some drug he's addicted to.

We finally reach the blackjack tables and find two seats together at a twenty-five dollar minimum table. I have never played at a table with this high a minimum, but my father insisted. There are two other people at the table and they look at us as we take our seats. One of them is a hefty older gentleman probably around my father's age. The other is a decent looking woman probably in her forties. My father gives me three hundred dollar bills.

"No, no, no, I have money."

"Don't be silly son, take it, it's not like I'm gonna need it." I wish he would refrain from the death comments, it fucking depresses me.

"Alright." I take the cash.

"Oh and that's your inheritance so don't blow it all in five minutes." He looks at me and laughs. I shake my head and think to myself, since when did my father get such a dark sense of humor? He takes three hundred out for himself and we set our cash on the table.

The dealer takes my cash and yells "exchanging three hundred." Then she sets grabs and sets down eight twenty-five dollar chips and one hundred dollar chip down in front of me. She does the same with my father's three hundred.

We both lay a twenty-five dollar chip down to play the next hand. My father gets a jack and I get a two, of course. The dealer turns a seven. My dad's second card is an ace, twenty one, unbelievable, and he wins thirty-seven fifty. My second card is a nine and I double down. My next and final card is a six, seventeen, not too bad. Worst case scenario is the dealer flips a ten or face card and we push, unless she flips an ace, then I'm screwed. The dealer takes a second card, flips it over, and of course, it's a fucking ace, eighteen, I lose. My dad laughs and I look at him and shake my head.

"Un-fucking-believable." I say as the dealer takes my two twenty-five dollar chips and adds them to her huge house stack.

"Welcome to Vegas son." He says and then smiles.

We set another twenty-five dollar chip down to play the next hand. An hour later we leave the table. I'm three hundy down and the old man is two hundy up. He gives me a hundred and we head to the dollar Wheel of Fortune slot machines. I lose twenty bucks in two minutes. My father hits three spins on his second pull, of course. He spins the wheel and it stops on one hundred. I look at him like are you kidding me?

"You got a four leaf clover up your ass or what old man?"

"It looks like it, but if you don't stop losing, it won't matter." He laughs and I can't help but laugh myself. Just being here with him, win or lose, it doesn't matter, what matters is that we are together, having a great time, and I don't want it to end.

When it is all said and done my father walks away with an extra fifty bucks and I walk away with zip, zilch, nothing but lint in my pockets. We head to the bar to get a couple beers.

We sit there and each throw a twenty dollar bill into the video poker machines that are built into the bar in front of us, which makes our beers free but not really. In the end the four beers total we drink will cost us forty bucks; nothing is free in Vegas.

"So I was thinking that we should see a show." My father says.

"Oh yeah, which one?"

"Well I've always wanted to see the Cirque du Solei show Love, you know the Beatle's one?"

"Yeah I've heard of it."

"Well, I got us a couple of tickets for the eight o'clock show tonight."

"How long have you been planning this?"

"Well after you said you were coming up I reserved the room and the tickets online."

"How did you know I was gonna come with you?"

"I had a hunch and even if you didn't I was gonna come here anyway." I chuckle. "So you want to grab some dinner before the show?"

"Yeah, what do feel like?"

"I hear the buffet here is pretty good."

"Well, let's check it out."

We get up from our seats at the bar and head to the buffet. There's no one in line at the buffet which is strange, even though it's a Monday night. My father pays the twenty bucks each; he still won't let me pay for anything, but I think it's his way of making up for the past ten years that he missed out buying me shit. We head in, grab a plate, and load it up with as much shit as we can. I'm talking mash potatoes, macaroni and cheese, short ribs, orange chicken, green beans, and a couple dinner rolls.

After we finish our first plates we head back for round two. This time it's a big juicy thick slice of prime rib and a salad; you have to get your greens. After we kill that we head back for round three, dessert. My father goes for the cheesecake and I go for the double chocolate brownie, which I make even more amazing with some soft serve vanilla ice cream oozed on top of it and then I top it off with some chocolate syrup and some chopped nuts.

After dessert our stomachs are bursting and we literally have to adjust our belts accordingly. We sit there, slouched in our chairs, just exhausted, our stomachs yelling at us saying what the hell is wrong with you two, we told you to stop after the first plate. After a good twenty minutes of food digestion we're able to stand, which we do. We high tail it out of the buffet before someone realizes how much food we ate and they decide to ban us for life.

We walk to the Mirage Hotel and Casino where the Cirque show Love is being performed. We are a tad early so we head to a couple slot machines and toss in a hundred each. We grab a cocktail server that walks by and order a couple beers. She returns ten minutes later, which is a decent time considering they usually take their sweet ass time. My father tips her a twenty and tells her to hurry back with two more. She smiles and we smile back. We drink our beers and both blow our hundreds on the machines that we are playing. She returns with round two and we hammer them down with the quickness. Then we head into the show, which was amazing.

After the show we head back to Caesar's and decide to hit the craps table for a bit. After an hour I am down two hundred and my father is up three hundred; lucky bastard, but I guess he deserves it considering. Around eleven thirty my father tells me that he is beat and he wants to head back up to the room and laydown. I can't believe he has lasted this long. He is a goddamn beast. He says I can stay and play if I want and I tell him no chance, I'm beat too.

When we get back up to the room my father pulls out his bong.

"Jesus dad, you brought that with us?"

"Of course, how else am I supposed to ease my pain?" My mind wanders to the scene in *Field of Dreams* where Kevin Costner hears the voice say ease his pain and all I can think about is Kevin Costner handing my father a bong and I laugh out loud. My father looks at me like did I just say something funny?

"What if we get pulled over?"

"I have cancer son relax; besides I have a medical marijuana prescription." He packs the bowl, lights it, takes a hit, and exhales. He offers it to me, I take it, and repeat what he just did. When the bowl is ashed we head to our rooms and pass out.

<u>CHAPTER FOUR</u>

I awake to the sound of my father banging on the door to my room. "Wake up son. We have to get going soon." He pauses, apparently trying to hear if I respond, because he starts up again with the banging after I don't. "Son, get up, get ready, we gotta go." He pauses again.

"Okay, okay, I'm up, I'm up."

"Be ready in thirty minutes… I got you a coffee by the way; it's out here getting cold."

"Okay." I yell and then I roll over and hug one of the pillows before I throw the covers off of me, stretch out my entire body, and slowly get out of bed. I walk over, open the door, and enter the living room of the suite. My father is sitting on the sofa drinking a coffee.

"Do you ever sleep?"

"I'll sleep when I'm dead."

 I glare at him. "That's not funny."

He smiles. "Yeah, I know. I've said that most of my adult life I guess it has a more personal meaning now."

"Ya think?" I grab my coffee from the desk it's sitting on and take a drink. "I'm gonna shower."

"Okay, but you only have twenty-five minutes."

"What's the rush?"

"We have an appointment at ten."

"What appointment?" I take another drink.

"I'll tell ya in the truck, now go shower."

"Alright." I head back into the bedroom and then into the attached bathroom. I shower, dry off, get dressed, finish my coffee, grab my pack, and we head out of the room. My father has already checked us out via the check-out option on the television, so we just head to the truck, throw our packs in the back, and hit the road.

"So where are we going?"

"I'll tell ya in a bit, just enjoy the ride."

Him not telling me where we are going gives me a very uneasy feeling and I begin to worry as we leave the highway and head down a gravel road. Five minutes later all I can see is what looks like an airport hangar and runway out in the middle of nowhere Nevada.

"Here we are." My father says as he points to a huge sign

that says skydiving with an arrow pointed in the direction that my father just turned. I quickly look over at him.

"Oh hell no."

"Oh hell yes son. We are goin' skydivin'."

"Um, what do you mean by we? You gotta mouse in your pocket?"

He laughs. "Come on son, don't be a chicken shit, jump out of a plane with me."

"Are you even supposed to do that? I mean, that can't be good for you can it?"

He parks the car, turns the ignition off and looks at me. "Son, within the hour I'll be jumping out of one of these planes with some stranger strapped to my back. I'm doin' it with or without ya, but I would rather do it with ya, so man up Mr. Zen lunatic and let's get crazy."

Damn I can't believe my father just called me out like that. I guess I better practice what I preach. "Alright, let's do it." I reluctantly say.

We get out of the truck and head to the main office. After filling out some liability forms, paying, and getting a little skydiving lesson, we head up in a small propeller plane. As the plane rises all I can think about is how the hell did I go from a cozy warm bed at Caesar's Palace to flying in a plane about to jump out of it in just under two hours? When we reach the correct altitude we prepare for the jump. The instructors strap us in so our backs are glued to their fronts.

"You wanna go first?" My father yells.

"No, you go right ahead." I yell back.

"Okay, see ya on the ground."

How the hell did I let him talk me into this? His instructor prepares them for their jump and poof, their gone. My instructor prepares us for our jump and I look down and I can see the black ball that is my father and his instructor free falling to the ground. Then all I hear is one, two, three, and all of a sudden I am falling towards the earth like a rogue meteor, screaming like a little girl. But then after a good minute I stop screaming and it is eerily quiet.

I look around at the Nevada landscape and I am totally relaxed and in an insane meditative state and then the instructor pulls the chute open breaking my meditation and we begin to float towards the ground. I take a deep breath thankful that the chute opened and then look around. There is nothing but a huge city isolated in the middle of nothing, a desert, and it looks strange from up here. At that moment I think to myself, what were the people thinking when they built this city out here? What made them stop at this location and just decide to build a gambling paradise? The thought leaves my mind as I notice we are getting close to the ground. A minute later we land on our feet and the ride is over. Holy shit that was insane and totally awesome. My father is waiting there for me not too far away and after the instructor detaches from me I run towards him the best that I can in this ridiculous outfit. When I reach him I give him a huge hug.

"Wow, what a trip that was." I say.

"Yeah, that was nuts, but I'm glad you did it son."

"And I'm glad you convinced me to do it dad. Now can we get back to the truck, I think I pissed myself."

He laughs, but I wasn't joking. We get out of our suits and jump back into the truck. I still can't believe we did that.

"Hungry?" He asks.

"Starving."

"Alright, well let's eat and gas up before we head up through Nevada, there aren't a lot of places to stop up there."

"Sounds good."

We head to the nearest truck stop and eat a huge breakfast, even though it's just about noon. We grab some drinks for the cooler and a few snacks for the road. Then we gas up and head north on highway 93, straight up through the nothingness that most of Nevada has to offer.

"So we have several hours and nothing to look at you wanna tell me now what you've been up to these past ten years?" I say as we continue north.

"What do you want to know?"

"Everything." I grab a water from the cooler, open it, and take a drink.

"Well let's see, when I saw you last I was working at the Daily Sun, the newspaper in Flagstaff if you remember."

"Yeah I remember that."

"Well I stayed there for about two more years after that and then I had a bit of a falling out with the boss so I quit. Then I basically just sat around for a few months reading and writing a few freelance pieces here and there. One of the books I read during that time was *A River Runs Through It*, the book you so thoughtfully got me for my birthday." My father looks at me and smiles. I shake my head and smile back. "After I read that book I just got this bug up my ass and I headed up there like I told you the other day. I stayed up there for a few weeks and then headed back to Flagstaff. I thought about just selling the house and moving up there but I never pulled the trigger on that idea. Then I found a job teaching journalism and creative writing at a local high school and I've been doing that ever since, well since I got the cancer anyway. It was a sweet gig and it allowed me to spend my summers up in Montana fishing the Big Blackfoot.

"What about the ladies?"

"Well before Sarah there were a couple of ladies but nothing serious." My father grabs a bottle of water from the cooler, opens it, and takes a drink.

"So tell me about Sarah."

"Well I told you how we met the other night. How I saw her at the jukebox and then she waved us over. Well we ended up talking the rest of the night and I found out that she worked in the financial aid office at the University of Montana. I also discovered that she loved to fly fish and we spent the majority of time talking about that. Anyway, I get her number and we had dinner the next night, which I think I told you already. At dinner she told me that she was married once before and that she had a daughter, Jessica, which I also told you about the other night."

"So how old is she?"

"Jessica or Sarah?"

"Sarah, I·think you told me Jessica is twenty-five."

"Yeah, that's right. Um, Sarah is forty-nine."

"Younger, nice."

"Shit son, when you're in your forties or fifties or hell even your sixties it's all pretty much the same."

"I guess that's true." I grab a small bag of Cool Ranch Doritos, open it, take a chip out, and eat it. I offer the bag to my father and he takes a couple chips from the bag and eats them. "So how was it when you went back to Flagstaff, I mean long distance relationships kinda suck."

"Yeah, it was rough but we would Skype a lot and I went up during fall, winter, and spring breaks. It wasn't as bad as you might think."

"I'm happy for you dad, she sounds like an amazing woman."

"Oh she is son and I can't wait for you two to meet. I have told her all about you, at least all that I know."

My happiness for my father fades and I am saddened by the fact that I did not do much, or anything for that matter, to keep in contact with him over the past decade.

"I know I said it before, but I am really sorry about that dad, I don't know why I couldn't get over the divorce or why I…" I was going to say hate you, but I didn't hate him, so I pause to search for a better word to describe my feeling towards him during that time. "…I despised you so much." He looks at me.

"You had your reasons. You were a kid and kids want both of their parents around and I left. I tried to explain it to you when you were a teenager but the rebellious side of you wouldn't listen or just didn't care. But like I said before, you were young and pissed, but now we can attempt to mend our broken relationship and make-up for lost time, while there is still time. And like I said before, that is why I asked you to come on this trip with me."

I look at him, tears welling up in my eyes. "I'm glad you asked me to come and I am glad I came and I am honored to be your best man." With that being said the conversation ended and I turned on the radio and we jammed out to Lynyrd Skynyrd as we continued to drive north through the Nevada wasteland.

Just as the sun begins to set we reach Interstate 80 in northern Nevada and pass under it staying on highway 93, which will take us all the way to Missoula. An hour later we leave Nevada and enter Idaho. About ten minutes into Idaho we almost die.

There are zero lights out here except for the occasional farmhouse, which freaks me out. The thought of getting a flat tire or something else happening to my dad's truck, which would make us have to go to one of those farmhouses and ask to use the phone because there is zero cell service out here is something I would rather not do. All I can think about is the

Texas Chainsaw Massacre and that it would be just our luck that the farmhouse we go to is the home of a family of chainsaw wielding cannibalistic psychopaths. My point is that it is pitch black out here and in the darkness of night it is hard to see the road, let alone what is along the road. My father's truck doesn't have the best headlights either, which adds to the problem. Anyway, as we drive in the dark in Southern Idaho I see a herd of elk to our left, headed away from us on the southbound side of the highway.

"Oh shit, watch out." I yell.

"I see it, it's going the other way." My father replies. And he is right, but I don't think he saw what I saw.

"Did you see all of his friends?"

"His friends?"

"Yeah, there were at least a dozen elk in front of him."

"No, I only saw him."

"Judas Priest we could have died." I turn and look out the back window to see them, but they are gone. I turn back around. "If we would have been there thirty seconds earlier we would have driven right smack into that herd of elk."

"Well I guess we were lucky I was driving over the speed limit. Hey if we get stopped by the Highway Patrol tell them that story and they might feel sorry for us and let us go with a warning." He looks at me and smiles.

"That might work."

"Not a chance son, not a chance."

A short time after our near death experience we reach Twin

Falls, Idaho and stop for the night. We get a room with two queen beds at the Days Inn right off of highway 93 and Interstate 84. We are starving so we decide to just walk next door to the restaurant inside the Flying J Travel Plaza to grab some dinner. We are given a booth right by the front door along with a couple menus. Our waitress shows up seconds later with two ice waters. She is nothing like Raelynn back in Flagstaff. She is older, probably in her late forties, but she could be younger. I feel the years have not been too kind to her. She is wearing glasses and her auburn hair is put up in a messy bun. She walks away as we peruse our menus.

"So what looks good" My father asks.

"I don't know, I'm leaning towards the bacon cheeseburger."

"You can never go wrong with a bacon cheeseburger."

"So what are you thinkin'?" I ask him.

"I'm feelin' the steak and eggs."

"Good choice."

At that moment our waitress, whose name tag reads Connie appears in front of us. "You gentleman ready to order?"

We continue to look at our menus.

"I think we are Connie." My father says. "Son, go ahead."

"I'll have the bacon cheeseburger with fries please." I hand her the menu.

"How would you like your burger cooked?"

"Medium rare please."

"Okay and for you sir?" She looks at my father.

He is still looking at his menu, but then closes it. "I will have the steak and eggs please. The eggs over medium with a side of sourdough toast, extra toasted." He hands her his menu and she takes it after writing his order down.

"I will put that in...Oh and would you gentlemen like something besides water?" My father and I look at each other and I shake my head.

"You don't have any scotch do you?" My father jokes. She gives him an are you serious look and I chuckle a bit.

"No we don't sir." She didn't think it was funny.

"Okay, than just the waters are fine." She leaves and my father looks at me and smiles. "Well that one has no sense of humor."

"No she doesn't."

We sit in silence for a minute or so enjoying our waters and just relaxing.

"So dad I was wondering, did you write up a bucket list when you found out about the you know what?"

"Yeah, well I didn't write an actual list but I had some things I wanted to do."

"Like what?"

"Like skydive and see my son." He smiles and I smile back.

"Well I guess you can check those two things off the list."

"Yes I can."

"Anything else?"

"Not really, I guess just marry Sarah and get some more fly fishing in, that's about it. What about you?"

"What about me?"

"Well I know you're not dying, but is there something you've always wanted to do that you haven't got a chance to do yet?"

I take another drink of my water. "This week is about you dad not me."

"Oh don't give me that shit. What do you want to do? Give me something."

I think for a minute. "Well this might sound crazy, but I've always wanted to ride a bull."

My father's eyes get wide. "No shit."

"Yeah, ever since I was about ten. I remember I was flipping through the channels one day and I came across the PBR Championships and I thought it was so cool."

"Well let's do it."

I look at him like he's crazy. "Yeah sure let's do it." I say in a sarcastic tone.

"I'm serious son, let's go ride a bull."

I have never seen him so excited. He wasn't even this excited when we jumped out of that plane this morning.

"There is no way that I would let you get on a bull."

"Yeah I probably shouldn't do that, but you definitely should."

"Are you serious?"

"Absolutely and I think I know a place where you can do

it."

"How the hell do you know where a bull riding place is?"

"I've travelled every highway imaginable from Flagstaff to Missoula over the past eight years. I think I remember seeing a place in Jackson Hole, Wyoming." At that moment Connie shows up with our food. "What do ya say?"

"Let's eat and I'll think about it."

"Right on."

My father begins to cut into his steak and I take a huge bite of my bacon cheeseburger, which isn't too bad. We are halfway through our dinner and I can tell my father can't sit still and he finally breaks the silence.

"So what do ya say son?"

I shake my head and chuckle. "You really want me to ride a bull?"

"Hey you said it, not me. And yeah, before I die I would love to see my son try to ride a bull."

I shake my head again. "Really? You're really gonna play the cancer death card on this one?"

He shakes his head and smiles as he takes another bite of his steak. I think about it for a few more seconds.

"And then we can head up through the Tetons and Yellowstone. You talk about beautiful country, nothing beats the Tetons." He says.

"The Tetons?" I perk up.

"Yep. Ever seen'em?"

"No, but my buddy Max told me all about'em. He stopped

there on his way home from visiting his dad in South Dakota about a year ago. He said it was one of the most spiritual places he had ever been."

"Well then I guess it's set, you ride a bull, you see the Tetons, it's a win-win."

I shake my head again. "A win-win for who?"

"Both of us son, both of us...unless a bull sticks his horn up your ass, than it's just a win-win for me." He smiles.

I can't help but laugh. "Alright dad, let's find me a bull to ride."

He smiles even bigger this time and I think to myself that I'll ride a bull everyday if it will make him smile like that. We finish up our food, pay the bill, and then head back to the motel room. We watch the news for a bit, mainly to check the weather, and then we hit the sack. I need my rest; I have a date tomorrow in Jackson Hole, Wyoming with a bull.

CHAPTER FIVE

I awake to the sound of someone opening our motel room door and it is my father holding two coffees in a drink carrier and a bag of something.

"Rise and shine." He says as I rub my eyes and throw the covers over my head. "I have coffee and donuts." I throw the covers off of me and groan as I stretch my entire body. "I got you a maple bar and an apple fritter. I rub my eyes again and sit up in the bed. He hands me a coffee and takes a bear claw from the bag and then hands the bag to me.

"Thanks."

"No problem."

I reach into the bag and pull out one of the donuts without

looking at them and it's the apple fritter. I take a bite. I take another sip of my coffee as my father lies down on his bed.

"So what's the plan?" I ask.

"Well, its four hours to Jackson Hole, so I figure we hit the road, get some lunch when we get into town, and then go find a bull for you to ride."

"We're still doing that huh?"

"Oh you betcha." He says in his best Minnesotan accent, which is pretty spot on.

I finish off my apple fritter and then reach into the bag to attack the maple long john. "I take it you've already showered?"

"You heard me?"

"I think so, but I wasn't totally sure."

"Yeah, I'm ready to go when you are."

"Okay, I'll jump in the shower after I finish this and then we can head out."

"Sounds good."

He turns on the television and flips through the channels as I finish off my second donut and head to the bathroom to shower. Twenty minutes later I'm dressed and ready to go. I throw our packs in the back of the truck and hop in the passenger side while my father checks us out of the motel. He hops into the drives seat, starts the truck up and we head out of the parking lot. Then we jump on Interstate 84 headed east towards Pocatello, which is less than two hours away. When we reach Pocatello we merge onto Interstate 15 and head north towards Idaho Falls, which is about forty-five minutes away.

When we get to Idaho Falls we head east on highway 26 for forty minutes and then turn left onto highway 31, which turns into highway 33, which turns into highway 22, also called Teton Pass Highway. We meander back and forth through the Rocky Mountains. There is still snow on the sides of the highway and on the top half of the tree covered mountains. It is a breath-taking scene, Mother Nature at her finest. We drive through the small town of Wilson and then cross over the Snake River. Twenty minutes later we reach the outskirts of Jackson Hole, a beautiful town surrounded by the Rocky Mountains; the Tetons are just to the north. We turn left onto highway 191 and drive through town looking for a place to grab some lunch, and if my father has it his way, a place where I can ride a bull. I still don't think he can pull it off, but if he does somehow find a bull for me to ride then I guess I'll have to man up and ride it or at least attempt to.

I spot a place called Bubba's Bar-B-Que and suggest that we stop there for lunch, my father agrees. We head to the front counter and both order a pulled pork sandwich with a side of barbeque beans and a Diet Coke. About halfway through our meal my father gets up and walks over to the front counter. He starts talking to the heavy set guy that took our order and then returns.

"What was that about?"

"Oh I was just asking that guy if he knew where we could do a little bull ridin'."

"And what did he say?"

"He said he might know of a place. He said he would make a few calls and get back to me."

I shake my head. "You really want to see me get bucked off a bull don't you?"

He smiles. "Of course not son, I wanna see you ride that son-of-a-bitch for eight seconds and then hop off of it like it was nothin' and shout out a big yee-haw."

I laugh. "Yeah like that's gonna happen."

"You never know. Even the sun shines on a pig's testicles at some point."

I look at him funny. "I don't think that's the right saying dad."

"Oh well whatever, it just means you might get lucky."

"Yeah dad, I know what it means." I chuckle and shake my head. At that moment the guy behind the counter appears.

"Here ya go." The man hands my father a slip of paper. "Call that number and the guy should be able to set up a ride for ya."

My father looks at the number on the slip of paper and then looks at the guy. "Thank you sir it's much appreciated."

"No problem, just make sure you two don't kill yourselves." He walks back behind the counter and my father looks at me and laughs.

"Alright boy let's finish up, you have a bull to ride."

I look at him and shake my head. "Unbelievable." I say as the fear of death by bull horn up the ass suddenly hits me like a bolt of lightning.

We finish our lunch and then head back to the truck. My father calls the number. "Hello, is this Travis?...It is, great. My name is John and I was told that you might be able to help me out...Well my son has always wanted to ride a bull and I thought this would be the perfect time and place...He's twenty-eight...Yeah, he's in great shape...I assume he does..." He looks at me. "You have insurance right?"

"Yeah." The fear is building.

"Yeah he has insurance...Yeah that's fine...Okay." He grabs a pen and writes something down on the back of the slip of paper with the phone number on it. "Okay, great, see ya in a bit." He hangs up the phone and looks at me and I just shake my head. "Travis said we can come on over, he has a ranch not too far from here with a couple bulls and all the gear you need and he's only charging us three hundred."

I get wide-eyed. "Three hundred dollars? To ride a bull for two seconds?"

"It's eight seconds and he said you could ride it as many times as you wanted within an hour."

"So this is happening?"

My father smiles and nods. "Yep, unless you chicken out."

"That's a possibility."

"Oh this is going to be good." He says as he puts the truck in gear and drives off quite possibly to my final resting place.

We get to the ranch in fifteen minutes and I see a man I assume is Travis standing in front of what appears to be a small rodeo arena. We exit the truck and make our way over to him. He looks like he might be in his mid to late thirties and he has a short stubbly beard. He is wearing typical cowboy attire, Wrangler jeans, a black button-up long sleeve shirt, black cowboy boots, and a black Stetson hat.

"You must be John." Travis says in a country twang. They shake hands.

"I am and this is my son Andrew." I shake his hand and it's a firm handshake to say the least. He might have broken two of my fingers.

"Nice to meet ya."

"Same here." I say as he looks me dead in the eye.

"So you wanna ride a bull huh?" At that moment I completely regret telling my father that I wanted to do this.

"Well I'm not so sure now."

"Ah it'll be fine, ya jus hold on tight, stay loose, and enjoy the ride." He laughs knowing full well it isn't that easy and then my father joins him in laughter. "Alright let's git the business out of the way so we can have some fun. I got a liability form here for ya to sign and date."

"Liability form?" I say.

"Yeah, jus in case my bull tramples you to death or you take a horn to the nuts, stuff like that." Travis hands me the form and my eyes are open as wide as they can possibly be and all I can hear is my father laughing his ass off. I'm frozen with fear, standing there with the form in my hand, my arm still straight out. "Ah I'm kiddin' man, but seriously, this is dangerous business, but don't worry I have a vest and a helmet and even a cup if you want it."

"Sure." I lower my arm and turn towards my father. "Why does it seem that I'm filling out liability forms every day on this trip?"

He smiles at me. "Cause you are."

He and Travis both laugh as I head to the truck to sign and date the form while my father pays the man. I return and hand the liability form back to Travis who scans it to make sure I actually signed it.

"Alright, let's go get you set up with some gear and then we'll go meet Black Death."

"Black Death?"

"Yeah, that's the bull's name, but don't worry he's a sweetheart." They both laugh and I suddenly feel my heart begin to race.

Travis gives me a protective vest and a helmet to put on, which I do. He offers me a cup but I decline, I have no idea whose nuts have been in that thing and I really don't want crabs or whatever else I can catch from a used nut cup. He also gives me a pair of leather gloves so I don't rip the skin off of my hands while I try to hold on to the rope. After I get all the gear on Travis takes us to the pen where I will get on Black Death and go for my ride.

"Lemme go grab him and load him up for ya, I'll be right back."

"Okay." My father says. He smiles and looks at me. I am

frozen and noticeably terrified. My father turns and grabs me
by the shoulders with both hands. "Son, you can do this. You
are an animal, a fucking wild man, that bull is your bitch." I
am starting to get a little pumped up now. "And remember,
you ride the bull, the bull doesn't ride you." At that moment I
realize that I've heard him say something similar to that
before.

"That's part of your driving speech isn't it?" I say.

"What do you mean?" He plays dumb.

"When you were teaching me how to drive during one of
my visits you told me that I control the car, the car doesn't
control me."

"Yeah, so, it's still true."

At that moment I hear the clanking and snorting of Black
Death being loaded into the pen we are standing next to and I
turn and jump back a bit.

"Alright Andrew climb up here." I climb up to the top of
the metal fence as does my father. Black Death is just that, a
huge black beast of a bull with snot hanging from his nose or
snout or whatever you call it, and I swear he just winked at
me. "Okay now straddle him." I do as he says and I can feel
every muscle in this bull's body between my legs. "Okay, now
grab the rope." I do as he says. "Okay, now when I open this
gate just squeeze him with your legs and keep your upper boy
loose and just hold on as long as you can. And when you get
bucked off just get up fast and run to the nearest fence and
climb it, I will distract him, okay?" I take a deep breath and

exhale.

"Alright, let's do this." I tighten my grip and wait. Travis opens the gate and Black Death shoots out of the gate and into the arena. I squeeze my legs as tight as I can and hold on to the rope as tight as I can but it's pointless. I get tossed within two seconds. When I hit the ground I do as Travis said and I run my ass to the fence and climb over it like a jackrabbit running from a wolf. I look in the arena and Travis is wrangling Black Death back up.

"Well at least you didn't get a horn up the ass." My father yells from down the fence.

"Thanks dad." I am totally pumped up now. The adrenaline is racing mad crazy through my body like water through a turbine. "Hey Travis, get that bull back in the pen I want another crack at him." Travis and my father don't believe their ears and Travis yells out a "yee-haw" and my father yells out a "hell yeah", which I think is the same thing. Travis loads Black Death back into the pen and I climb the fence and get back on him. The adrenaline is bursting out of my body. I take my helmet off and toss it to the ground next to my father's feet.

"What are ya doin'?" Travis asks.

"Yeah son, what are ya doin'?" my father repeats.

"Gimme your hat." I raise my right arm towards Travis.

"I don't think that's too good an idea." Travis says.

"Yeah son, don't be crazy."

"Just gimme the hat, if I'm gonna ride this bull I wanna

ride it like a cowboy."

"Alrighty." Travis takes his black Stetson off and puts it on my head. I adjust it and then tighten my grip on old Black Death.

"When I say go, let us loose."

"You got it." I take a couple of big deep breaths, tighten my grip again, and then I just focus and visualize the ride and then I say it.

"Alright, go." Travis opens the gate and old Black Death shoots out of the gate like a fucking bullet. He bucks once and I'm still on. He spins and I'm still on, but the hat flies off. He bucks again and I fly and flip over his head like a goddamn gymnast hitting the vault. I can see sky then dirt then sky then dirt. I finally hit the ground but I can't move, at least not until old Black Death comes after me and then I get up and out of there like a cat who was thrown in a bathtub full of water. Once I am over the fence I check my body for any blood or exposed bones, but I'm fine, just a little sore. My father runs over to me.

"Holy shit son, you okay?"

"Yeah, I'm fine."

"Holy shit, that was insane. You flipped over that bull like a goddamn ragdoll, I thought you were dead." He is going nuts.

Travis comes over after he pens up Black Death. "That was a nice little run."

"How long was it?" I ask.

"Shoot, I'd say about four seconds, which ain't bad at all for a rookie.

"Yeah, not too bad for a California surfer boy." My father adds.

"Y'all from California? Holy shit then strike that, four seconds is real good, real good. You wanna give him another go?"

"No, no, I'm good, twice was enough." I put my hands on my lower back and try to stretch it out.

"Alright, well just hand over the vest and you're free to go."

"What about the gloves?"

"You keep'em, you earned'em."

"Cool, thanks Travis."

"Yeah thanks Travis we really appreciate you accommodating us on such short notice." My father adds.

"No problem, money's money and I love watchin' rookies ride, nothin' on TV can even compare."

"Yeah I bet." My father agrees. "Well Travis thanks again, we'll see ya."

"You guys have a safe trip wherever you're headed."

And with that we climb back in the truck and head out, back towards highway 191. We stop at a gas station to fill the tank up and so I can use the bathroom, for more than one reason. Then we jump back on highway 191 and head north towards the Tetons.

We reach the entrance to Grand Teton National Park

twenty minutes later without having to pay because my father already has an annual pass to the national parks. We park in the Jenny Lake parking lot and get out. We decide to take a walk down the trail that goes along the southern bank of the lake.

"Man I wish I would have brought a couple fishing poles. My father says.

"Yeah, that would have been sweet. What kind of fish do you think are in here?" I point to the lake.

"I have no idea." We walk in silence for a little bit before I start the conversation back up. The majestic snow covered peaks of the Grand Tetons are right in front of us and I can see now what Max was talking about. The air is so clean here and it's almost like a dream.

"So are you going to take me fly fishing when we get to Missoula?"

"You better believe it. We can fish the Big Blackfoot on Friday and then the wedding is Saturday."

"Sounds like a plan. So how many people are going to be at the wedding?"

"Well there is Sarah and I and you and Jessica and Sarah's parents and Jim and a couple other friends of ours. It will be a small ceremony."

"So are you two getting married in a church or what?" At that my father smiles.

"Yeah, our church, the Big Blackfoot."

"What does that mean?"

"We're getting married on the bank of the Big Blackfoot River, right behind the house."

"That's awesome dad. It should be one hell of a ceremony."

"I think it will be. Hell I know it will be."

"We should head back to the truck if we plan on seeing Old Faithful before dark."

"Well, I was thinking that it would be cool if we camped here for the night, we do have a day to kill. What do you think?"

"Yeah, let's do it? Do we have a tent?"

"No, but I have an air mattress and a couple sleeping bags in the back of the truck. We can just sleep under the stars."

"Yeah, that sounds awesome."

We turn and head back towards the Jenny Lake parking lot. We get back to the truck just as the sun disappears behind the Grand Tetons. We remove the truck bed cover and I fold it up while my father inflates the air mattress with one of those battery powered portable inflators. The air mattress takes up most of the truck bed. We unroll the two sleeping bags and lay them on top of the air mattress. At that moment a park ranger approaches us.

"How are we doin' this evening?" He asks.

"We're good, how are you doin? My father says.

"I'm great. You gentlemen planning on staying the night?"

"Yeah, we were just going to sleep in the back of the truck here, if that's okay?"

"Well, we don't allow people to sleep in the parking lot, but you are welcome to drive right over there…" He point to the campground behind us and we look. "…and grab one of those campsites for the night if you like." We look back at the ranger.

"And how much is that gonna run us?" I ask.

"Twenty-five."

"That's fine." My father says as he grabs his wallet out of his back pocket, pulls out a twenty and a five, and hands it to the ranger.

"We also have bundles of wood for ten bucks, if you guys want to make a fire." My father looks at me and I nod.

"Yeah, we'll take a bundle." My father takes a ten out of his wallet and hands it to the ranger.

"I'll bring the wood over to you in a few minutes."

"Okay, sounds good. So we just take any open site?" My father asks.

"Yeah, any empty site is fine."

"Okay." I close the tailgate. We jump in the truck, exit the parking lot, and find a campsite not too far into the campground. My father parks the truck so we can sit on the tailgate and enjoy the fire. We hop out and I drop the tailgate back down. My father fixes the sleeping bags that had slid off the air mattress on the drive from the parking lot. We sit on the tailgate and wait for the ranger, who shows up fifteen minutes later. I search around for some kindling while my father constructs a tee-pee out of a few pieces of wood from the small bundle. I return with a good handful of small sticks and hand them to my father. He places them under the makeshift wood tee-pee and lights a few of them with his lighter. The kindling catches fire and slowly but surely ignites the wood tee-pee.

We sit back up on the tailgate and enjoy the heat coming off of the fire. We haven't eaten anything since our barbeque lunch, but there is nothing around here. So we just eat the leftover snacks that we have, which consists of a bag of Cool Ranch Doritos, a bag of Funyuns, two pieces of teriyaki beef jerky, and two Snickers bars. After "dinner" we sit in silence for a bit staring at the fire and just enjoying the great outdoors. Then my father decides to question me about my love life, or lack thereof.

"So, you're twenty-eight and no girlfriend, what's up with that?"

"I don't know, I don't really try that hard. Plus, I'm super busy with work and I don't really have time for a relationship."

"There is always time for love son."

"Yeah, well I guess I just haven't been paying much attention."

"Well you should. Being in love is our greatest gift. Have you ever been in love?"

"Once."

"Details?"

"Do we really have to do this?"

"No, we don't have to, but I'd like to know."

I think about telling him I really don't want to talk about it, but I feel I owe it to him for some crazy reason. "Alright, her name is Emily. I met her during the first week of my first year at Long Beach State, which was my junior year of college. I got to my Modern Philosophy class early and took a seat in the front." My father cuts me off.

"The front? You sat in the front on purpose?" He sounded surprised.

"Yeah, I always tried to sit in the front, when people are in front of me it distracts me. I like to pretend it is just me and the professor, it helps me concentrate."

"Interesting."

"Yeah, So I was sitting there right when class was about to begin and this girl sits down right next to me."

"Nice. So she must have thought you were this smart good-looking guy then."

"Well not exactly, at least I don't think so. The class filled up pretty quickly after I sat down and since no one liked to sit in the front, except for me apparently, those were the only open seats left. She didn't have much of a choice. Anyway, after class she told me that she didn't know if she could handle this class so I told her that I could help her if she wanted some help and she said yeah. So I gave her my number and then she sent me a text that night saying that she thought she might drop the class. I told her not to and that I would help her study."

"See son, you do have some game."

"I don't know if it was game, I was just being nice."

"Yeah, that's game." He says.

I laugh. "Yeah, well she made the first move about two weeks later because I didn't, so not too much game here dad."

"But you got the girl and that's all that matters."

"Yeah, I got her and then I lost her several months later."

"What happened?"

It takes me a few seconds to answer. "Mom died."

"Shit." He says, instantly regretting the question.

"Yeah, she tried to be there for me but I just lost it, I quit school, and then I just disappeared into the L.A. scene and she just gave up. When I came out of it, it was too late. She had already moved on. I was devastated, but it was my own fault so…"

"It wasn't your fault son. You lost your mother, that's tough to deal with. People deal with death in different ways, it's not like anyone is prepared for it, especially when it's a sudden death of a parent at a young age."

"Yeah, well I didn't deal with it how I should have."

"How should you have dealt with it?"

"I should have let Emily comfort me. I shouldn't have dropped out of school. I shouldn't have just disappeared."

"But you did and everything happens for a reason son, believe it or not. Look at me. The circumstances behind me going to Montana and eventually meeting Sarah. Do you know what the odds are of us meeting in that bar on that night?"

"Astronomical?"

"You better believe it, but it was supposed to happen, it was meant to be. Maybe you and this Emily girl just weren't meant to be or maybe you just weren't meant to be then. Do you know what she's up to now?"

"Yeah, she's married."

"Oh, well then she isn't the one, she was just the first one. Your one true love is out there somewhere son, you just have to believe and one day you will run into her and your heart will explode and you will know and you will forget all about that Emily girl."

I smile and chuckle. "I hope so dad, being single is cool, but I don't want to die alone."

"No you don't son and I should know that better than anyone. I am truly blessed, even though the cancer has a hold of me I have people around me that make it easier to deal with. I couldn't imagine having cancer and being alone, that would suck big time."

"Yeah it would." I agree.

The last of our wood is burning out so we decide to call it a night and hit the sack. It has been a long day and we are exhausted. My father puts the fire out and I climb into my sleeping bag. My father jumps up into the truck bed, then onto the air mattress, and then into his sleeping bag. We fall asleep to the symphony of unseen insects and the smell of burned wood.

CHAPTER SIX

I awake to the rising sun from the east illuminating our natural surroundings. I rub my eyes open and I am in awe by what is right in front of me, the Grand Tetons. The spectacular jagged peaks are covered in snow and the sun is shining on them like a spotlight on an opera singer. At the same time, Jenny Lake is sparkling and the entire scene is surreal. My father is still asleep, which is a first on this trip. He is usually already up with coffee and donuts in hand. I look and him and I think about all the traveling we have done over the past couple of days and all the craziness we have gotten into and I hope he isn't running himself ragged, which he probably is. At that moment he opens his eyes and looks right at me.

"What are you staring at son?" He catches me off guard, but I still manage to spit out something witty.

"Me in thirty years." I smile.

He laughs. "You can only hope to look this good son."

To that I laugh. "Yeah, except you look like Mr. Burns from the Simpsons after he spent an hour in the bathtub."

He laughs harder. "I have no comeback for that one...It's way too early in the morning for this shit."

I smile. "So what's the plan today?"

"I don't know, we have the entire day to kill. Maybe we should head back down to Jackson Hole and get a real breakfast slash lunch and then head back this way and check out Old Faithful up in Yellowstone. Then we can stop in Butte for the night before heading to Missoula tomorrow."

"Yeah, that sound like a great plan, I've never been to Yellowstone."

"Alright, well we're not in any hurry so we can chill for a bit and enjoy this insane landscape. Man the Tetons are beautiful."

"Yes they are."

We lie in the back of the truck for a good hour enjoying the beauty around us and then we hit the road. We take highway 191 south back to Jackson Hole and stop at a local diner for some real food. I get a Denver omelet and a short stack of pancakes. My father gets the steak and eggs again with a side of grits. After we eat we drive around Jackson Hole for a little bit just checking out what the town has to offer and then we jump back on highway 191 and head north back towards the Tetons.

Two and a half hours later we reach Yellowstone National Park and the entrance to Old Faithful. We park and notice that there is hardly anyone there. We hop out of the truck and walk over to see the natural wonder that is Old Faithful. It's strange, I feel like everyone that is born in America knows what Old Faithful is, but how many people have actually seen it? I remember learning about it in elementary school but I don't remember why.

We approach the geyser and read on a sign that it can shoot anywhere from thirty-seven hundred to eighty-four hundred gallons of water to a height of a hundred and six to a hundred and eighty-five feet and last anywhere from one and a half to five minutes. When I read that, I hope that the next eruption is soon, because the sun is beginning to set. My hope is answered as the geyser erupts ten minutes after we get there. A huge gush of white water shoots up towards the sky and we are in awe. My father has apparently seen it before, but this is a first for me and I am blown away. The eruption lasts a good three minutes and when it ends we turn and head to the truck.

We Jump back on highway 191 north and reach Interstate 90 at Belgrade in just under three hours. We jump on Interstate 90 and head west. Thirty minutes later we roll into Butte, Montana and look for a place to crash. We find a Quality Inn and Suites just off of the interstate and check in. We head to the room and throw our packs on the beds and then head to a

Quiznos sandwich shop down the street. We grab a couple sandwiches and then head back to the motel room. We eat while we watch Sportscenter. My father calls Sarah and lets her know where we are and that we should be In Missoula around noon tomorrow. He hangs up after he tells her he loves her and we watch a little more Sportscenter before we hit the sack.

We are jolted awake the next morning by the sound of glass shattering. I look over at the digital alarm clock and it is six in the morning on the dot. I jump out of bed, run to the window, and pull the curtain to the side. I look out the window and see a woman wielding a wooden baseball bat destroying an older model blue mustang. She has shattered the front windshield and is now taking her anger out on both headlights.

"Dad come over here, you gotta check this out."

My father gets out of bed, walks over next to me, and piers out the window. "Holy shit." He says as she walks to the rear of the car and starts smashing out the tail lights.

At that moment a guy wearing nothing but jeans runs over to the car and starts yelling. The woman sees him and swings the bat at his head. He jumps back and the bat misses his head by inches.

"Oh shit." I say as we continue to watch the scene unfold right in front of our eyes. The woman then starts bashing in the top of the trunk and the guy grabs her.

"Should we do something?" My father says to me.

"I don't think so, not unless he gets physical with her."

We continue to watch as the man tries to take the baseball bat away from her, which he does. He then raises the bat like he is going to hit her with it and my father heads towards the door.

"Wait, he lowered the bat dad, hold on."

My father returns to the window and the guy tosses the bat down the parking lot and they start arguing. From what I can hear the woman has apparently caught her husband or boyfriend with another woman.

After a few minutes of arguing the cops show up. The woman flips the guy off as one of the police officers grabs her and escorts her to the patrol car. The other officer stays with the guy and they start talking. We continue to look on, amazed at what we have just witnessed. After several minutes the officer that was talking to the woman walks over to the other officer that is still talking to the man. Then the guy walks away and the two officers walk back over to their patrol car and start talking to the woman. Apparently the guy is not going to press charges because the woman jumps in her car and takes off. Then the police officers do the same.

"Fuckin' Butte." My father says as he heads to the bathroom.

I lie back down on my bed and try to fall back asleep but there is no chance of that happening. My father enters the room and lies down on his bed.

"So, what shall we do now?"

I turn my head and look at him and he turns his head and

looks at me. "Showers and breakfast I guess."

He looks back at the ceiling. "Sounds good to me."

"So how far is it to Missoula from here?"

"Two hours tops." He says as he sits up in his bed and rubs his head with both hands.

"Okay." I say as I grab the television remote and press the power button. "You can shower first."

"Okay." My father stands up, grabs some clothes from his pack, and heads back into the bathroom. I flip through the channels looking for nothing in particular. I hear the shower turn on as I stop on Good Morning America. I set the remote down and wait for my turn in the bathroom.

My father exits the bathroom fifteen minutes later fully clothed minus shoes and socks. "It's all yours." He says as he dries his hair with his towel.

"Cool." I roll off the bed, walk over and get some clothes out of my pack, and then head to the bathroom. I take a shower and it feels amazing. The tepid water attacks my skin with the ferocity of a Gatling gun as it massages my shoulder and back muscles. Ten minutes later I turn off the water, grab my towel, and dry off. I put my clothes on, minus shoes and socks, and head back out to the main part of the motel room. My father is lying on his bed, shoes and socks now on, watching the same thing I was when I went to take a shower.

"Man that felt good, I needed that." I say as I dry my hair off with my towel.

My father looks at me. "Yeah, all we need now is some

coffee and some flapjacks." I look at him like he's crazy.

"Flapjacks? Did you really just say that?"

"What?"

"They're pancakes or quite possibly hotcakes, but not flapjacks."

"Why not?"

"Why not? Um, well because first of all that makes no sense, I mean what the hell does flapjack mean anyway?"

"Well flap is another term for flip and Jack is just a generic name for something like my name, John. So a flapjack basically means something that is flipped like a pancake." I shake my head.

"Of course you knew that."

He smiles. "Hey, you asked."

I chuckle. "Okay, let's go get some coffee and some flapjacks."

My father jumps off the bed and walks over to his pack and starts packing it up. I do the same.

"Oh, son?"

"Yeah?"

"What was the second thing?"

"What do you mean?"

"You said first of all, but never said a second thing."

I think about for a second. "Hell I don't know, it's just a figure of speech dad."

"If you say so."

We grab out packs and head out the door and to the truck.

The beat to shit mustang is still in the parking lot and I think to myself that's why I'm single. My father goes to the front office and checks us out and returns to the truck a couple minutes later. He hops in the driver's seat, starts it up, puts it into gear, and drives off. We stop at a local diner and grab some coffee and a couple stacks of flapjacks. After breakfast we get back on Interstate 90 and head west, Missoula is two hours away and I can't wait to get there and meet everyone.

As we zoom down the interstate at a constant speed of sixty-eight miles an hour, my father's trucks top speed, I start up a conversation.

"So what's the plan for the weekend?"

"Well, I thought we would do a little fishing tomorrow morning and then grab some lunch. Then we have our wedding dinner that night and then the wedding is Saturday afternoon."

"Is there a wedding reception after?"

"Well, we're just gonna go back to the house and eat and throw back a few cocktails, so I guess that's the reception, nothing fancy though."

"Cool. I can't wait."

"Yeah, me either."

We reach Deer Lodge and continue west on Interstate 90, Missoula is now only about an hour away. My father calls Sarah to let her know that we will be there soon. Then we spend the rest of the trip rocking out to some Rolling Stones and then my father tones it down with some John Denver. We reach the eastern outskirts of Missoula and exit Interstate 90 at ten after ten. My father pulls into the parking lot of a market and tells me to wait in the truck while he runs in to grab something real quick. He leaves the truck running and takes off, disappearing into the store.

He returns five minutes later holding a bouquet of various colored wildflowers in his left hand. He opens the driver's side door and hands me the flowers as he jumps in. He smiles and winks at me, puts the truck in gear, and takes off through the parking lot. We take a right onto highway 200 and head northeast. We reach the house five minutes later. Their house is a stone's throw from the Big Blackfoot River. It is a quaint little place, nothing fancy, but nice. There is one vehicle, a newer looking red pickup truck, in the driveway in front of the garage, which I assume is Sarah's. My father parks his truck right behind it and turns off the ignition.

"You ready?" He looks at me.

I look at him. "Let's do it."

We hop out of the truck, grab our packs and head towards the front door. I am still holding the flower so I hand them to my father after he opens the front door. We enter the house and are noses are immediately assaulted with the sweet smell of something that is sure to be delicious baking in the oven; my guess is chocolate chip cookies. We set our packs on the wood floor in the living room and then walk into the kitchen. A woman is standing behind the small island in the kitchen smiling. She is just as my father had described her, brown wavy hair, beautiful face, and a rockin' body.

"There they are." She says.

"Hey baby." My father walks over, hands her the flowers, and then gives her a huge hug and a kiss. He then turns and raises his right hand towards me. "This is my son Andrew." She hands the flowers back to my father and then walks out from behind the island and gives me a similar hug.

"It's so good to finally meet you Andrew." We end our embrace and I look at her.

"And it's good to finally meet you too Sarah."

She smiles and it lights up the room, my father was right, she's something else.

"So what's in the oven dear? It smells like your famous oatmeal chocolate chip cookies." My father says as he grabs a vase from one of the cabinets and begins to fill it with water from the kitchen sink. She turns to my father.

"And your nose would be correct sir. I thought I would make a special treat for this special occasion. Do you like oatmeal chocolate chip cookies Andrew?"

"Is the Pope Catholic?" I say smiling. My father laughs as he sets the water-filled vase on the kitchen island and places the flowers into it, fluffing them like a pillow only more gently.

"Well good, because I'm making three dozen." My eyes get big and my mouth begins to water. At that moment the oven timer goes off. "John, you want to show Andrew to his room while I take this batch out of the oven?"

"I can do that. Follow me son."

Sarah puts on an oven mitt. "Oh and John, the movers got here yesterday and loaded up the storage unit with your things."

"Okay, good."

"Oh and John?"

"Yes dear."

"Thank you for the beautiful flowers." She says with a smile.

"Anytime dear." My father replies as I follow him out of the kitchen and back into the living room. We grab our packs and I follow him again, this time to the guest bedroom that is just down the hall. "Here ya go, it looks like everything is set up and ready to go. You have pillows and blankets and there should be a towel in the hall bathroom for you to use. Why don't you get situated while I head to my room and empty my pack. Oh and just toss your dirty clothes on the hall floor and I will grab them and throw them in the wash with mine. And then I'll rendezvous with you back in the kitchen for some amazing oatmeal chocolate chip cookies."

"Sounds good dad, thanks."

"No need to thank me son, I should be thanking you."

And with that being said he heads down the hall to the master bedroom. I toss my pack on the bed and start grabbing all of my dirty clothes out of it and throwing them on the floor. Then I toss my pack on the floor near the foot of the bed and use my foot to push my dirty clothes out the door and into the hall. I close the door and lie down on the bed just to relax for a couple minutes.

I look around the room and the theme is obvious. There are a couple of paintings of rainbow trout swimming in a river on the far wall and I'm not sure if they were purchased or created by someone in this house. On the wall nearest to the hall there is a dresser with a stuffed brown trout on top of it. It is attached to two metal rods that are attached to a wood block base. I assume my father had caught the fish and then had a taxidermist mount it for him. It wasn't a big fish so I'm guessing that it must have been his first catch several years ago. I hear my father gather my dirty clothes up from the floor just outside the bedroom door and then walk off. The room does not have a typical closet but instead on the wall with the window in it there is a beautiful large armoire. I stretch out a bit and then sit up, then stand up, and head out of the bedroom and towards the kitchen where the smell of delicious cookies fills the air.

When I get to the kitchen there is a plate of a cookies on the island. Sarah is standing there flipping through a magazine. She looks up at me and smiles.

"Help yourself." She points to the cookies.

I grab one off of the plate and take a bite and they taste even better than they smell. Sarah grabs a napkin and hands it to me. "Thank you."

"Of course, would you like a glass of milk?"

"I would love a glass of milk."

She smiles again and then walks over, opens a cabinet, and takes out a tall glass. She then walks over to the refrigerator, opens it, and takes out a gallon of milk. She walks back over to the island, sets the glass down, opens the milk jug, and pours it into the glass. She slides the glass over to me and then returns the milk to the refrigerator. I take another bite of my cookie and then I take a drink of milk and I am transported back in time to when I was a kid and my mother did the same for me.

"So how was the drive up? She asks.

"It was great. We had an amazing time."

"So what kind of trouble did you guys get into?"

Before I could say anything my father enters the kitchen. "Don't answer that son. That is confidential information." My father smiles.

Sarah shakes her head. "Don't give me that John. I want to know what you guys did."

"We didn't do anything. We just jumped in the truck and drove up here."

She isn't buying one bit of that. "Yeah, sure."

"So what's the plan tonight?" My father tries to change the subject.

"Good try but I'm not telling you anything until you tell me what you two did these past few days."

"We'll tell you later sweetie, I promise."

She looks at him like she doesn't believe him. "You better."

He laughs. "Oh yeah and what if I don't?"

"Then I guess I'm gonna have to marry Jim on Saturday." My father shakes his head and I chuckle as I grab another cookie and take a bite. "Yeah that's gonna happen…So where's Jessica?"

"She should be over soon, she was headed over to David's to make sure everything is good to go for Saturday."

"Okay." My father looks at me as I stuff another cookie in my face. "David is the guy performing the ceremony. He's a good friend of ours and an ordained minister."

"Oh, cool." I say with a mouth full of deliciousness. I take another drink of milk to wash it down. Seconds later a thought hits me out of nowhere. "Um father?"

"Yes son."

"I just realized that I don't have anything nice to wear for the wedding."

"Yeah I know, my plan was to see if you could fit into anything I already have and it not then I was just gonna take you into town to find something. We're not gettin' crazy with the dress code, just jeans, a nice shirt, and a tie."

"Oh, okay, well let's go see if something fits and if not we can head into town. I wouldn't mind checking out Missoula if we have time." I suggest.

"Yeah, regardless of whether or not I have something that fits, we should definitely check out the town." I finish off another cookie and chug the rest of my milk. Then I follow my father to his bedroom closet to check out what he has. I look through the dress shirts that he has hanging in the closet and see one that doesn't look too bad and looks like it might fit me. It is solid navy blue, long sleeve, with a single pocket over the left breast. I try it on and it surprisingly fits like a glove. My father grabs a tie from his tie rack and hands it to me.

"Here, try this one with that shirt, it should work." It's a light blue paisley tie, which I toss around my neck and begin to tie. I am not the greatest at tying ties, which my father notices immediately. "Here son, let me get that for ya." He grabs both ends of the tie and starts tying if for me. A few seconds later he tightens it up towards my neck and adjusts the knot a tad. He looks at me. "Not too bad I must say. Let's check it out in the mirror." We walk out of the closet and over to a long mirror that is attached to a wall in the bedroom. I check myself out.

"You were right, not too bad. Is this okay for the wedding?"

"It's perfect. Now take it off and let's head into town for a bite before dinner."

"Okay."

I head to my room, take off the shirt and tie, and hang it up in the closet. Then I head back to the kitchen where my father is talking with Sarah, who still wants to know what we did on our trip up. He tells her we will spill the beans at dinner. They notice me walk in and both look at me.

"You ready son?"

"As ready as I'll ever be."

"Alright, let's go see what kind of trouble we can get into in the big town of Missoula."

Sarah looks at my father and shakes her head. "Just try to stay out of jail."

"We shall try." He says.

"And please be home by five."

"Can do, unless we're in jail."

She gives him a stern look and then looks at me. "Promise me you'll be back here at five and in one piece."

"I promise."

"We shall return at five and have a glorious family dinner." My father adds.

"Alright, get out of here you two and have fun."

My father gives Sarah a kiss and then we head out the front door to the truck and take off down the road towards Missoula.

After we grab a quick bite to eat at a local sandwich shop, my father drives me around the entire town of Missoula over the next three hours. He takes me by the University of Montana and shows me the football stadium and other parts of the campus. He takes me passed the Big Sky Brewery where we will be having the wedding dinner tomorrow night. He even takes me by the bar that he met Sarah at and the restaurant they had their first official date at.

Then before we head back to the house we stop at a liquor store and grab a case of Moose Drool Brown Ale, brewed by the local Big Sky Brewery. We get back to the house fifteen minutes before five. There is another car in the driveway.

"Oh good, Jessica's here. Ready to meet your future sister?"

"Yeah, let's do it." At that moment I think back to a week ago when I was sitting in my living room in Venice with Bear. I had no idea what my father was doing or where he was or who he was. And now I'm in Montana with him and my future step-mother, about to meet my future step-sister. It's amazing the twists and turns that life throws at you in such a short period of time. And then my thoughts travel back to the reality of why I am here and why this wedding is happening and I don't want to believe it and I don't want to think about it. My father is dying that's the reality of the situation, but I decide to bury that truth and try to enjoy the rest of the week with my new family.

We enter the house and make our way to the kitchen where Sarah and Jessica are sipping on glasses of red wine as food cooks in the oven and on the stove. The smells are incredible and my mouth begins to water immediately. They notice us walk in and both smile.

"There my two men are, both still in one piece." She looks at the clock on the stove. "And early, wow."

"A promise is a promise." I say as my father sets the case of Moose Drool on the counter.

"So Andrew, this is my daughter Jessica, Jessica this is John's son Andrew." We look at each other and smile. Jessica is a good looking woman with short brown hair and brown eyes.

"It's nice to finally meet you." She says.

"It's nice to finally meet you too." I go to shake her hand but she gives me a hug instead.

"Beer, son?" I look over at my father who is holding out a bottle of Moose Drool towards me."

"Of course." I take it from him, he sets one to the side for himself, and then he proceeds to stock the refrigerator with the remaining twenty-two beers. When he finally finishes he jumps up.

"I think we should eat outside tonight on the deck."

"But we already set the dining room table."

"That's okay, Andrew and I will move everything to the table outside real quick and then I will get a fire going in the fire pit. It will be nice."

"Okay, but dinner is about done, so get a move on."

"Yes ma'am." My father says like a soldier, even putting his right hand to his brow and saluting her. She shakes her head.

"I don't know why I'm even marrying you."

"Yes you do, cause you love me and I'm great in the sack." Jessica and I shake our heads, but laugh a little bit too.

"Really? Our kids don't want to hear that." Jessica and I shake our heads a little faster agreeing with Sarah.

I follow my father to the dining room to grab the plates, glasses, and silverware to transfer it outside. Ten minutes later the outside table on the back deck is set and a fire is going strong in the portable fire pit that my father set up right next to the table. We grab a couple fresh beers while the women dish up their plates and walk outside. We fix up our plates and join them a couple minutes later. We are all sitting there, this nice, new, small family unit, eating a delicious home-cooked meal outside as the Big Blackfoot serenades us in the background.

"So Andrew, you live in California is that right?" Jessica asks.

"I do."

"Whereabouts in California?" Sarah asks.

"I live in Venice, which is right by the beach not too far from downtown Los Angeles."

"With a girlfriend?" Sarah asks.

I laugh. "No, with a roommate."

"No girlfriend?" Sarah inquires.

"Nope." I take a bite of my chicken breast that is fabulously seasoned with several herbs and spices.

"And you are how old?" Sarah continues.

"I am twenty-eight."

"Is there at least a girl in the picture somewhere?" Sarah digs.

"Nope, not in the picture, not in the anything."

"Well there must have been someone at some point." Jessica joins her mother in the attack on my personal life.

"Well there was one about six years ago but that's history." I take a drink of my beer.

"Oh leave the boy alone, he'll find someone when he's

ready." My father interjects.

"We were just curious." Sarah says.

"It's fine, I don't mind the questions. I've just been working and living my life and there really hasn't been any women that have come along that have caught my eye so…"

"And what do you do for work?" Sarah asks.

"I work at a grocery store."

"Oh yeah, which one?" Jessica asks.

"Trader Joes, you know it."

"I've heard of it, I think there's one in Spokane."

"Yeah, it's a great company to work for."

The conversation stalls and we eat for a few minutes in silence enjoying the surrounding landscape and the hidden insect orchestra that is performing for us. The fire is raging and is keeping us perfectly warm on this somewhat cool spring evening.

"So, what kind of shenanigans did you two get into on your trip up?" Sarah says as she looks at both of us as does Jessica. She obviously did not forget and we didn't think she would.

My father decides to fess up. "Well we spent the first night in Vegas, did a little gambling, and went to the Cirque show Love, the one with the Beatle's music."

"Oh yeah, how was that?" Jessica asks as he looks at me and I answer.

"It was great, amazing performers and great music of course."

"And how much money did you lose?" Sarah glares at my father.

"I actually ended the night up, it was this one that lost money." He points at me.

I look at him and nod my head. "He's right about that, it was not my night that's for sure."

"Then the next day?" Sarah pushes for more.

"Then we drove up to Twin Falls." My father doesn't tell them about the skydiving, which I assumed he wouldn't. Sarah would kill him she knew he jumped out of a plane in his condition and just a few days before their wedding.

"And?" Sarah continues.

My father's mouth is full of chicken so I intervene. "And we almost hit a herd of Elk in southern Idaho." I look at my father to see if he cared if I shared that and he smiles at me silently thanking me for jumping in.

"Really?" Jessica says.

"Yep, if we would have been there thirty seconds sooner, bam…" I smack my hands together. "…we would have nailed them like a bowling ball into bowling pins."

"Jesus." Sarah says concerned.

My father calms her down. "But because of my steady speed limit driving we missed them and we are here now safe and sound eating this delicious meal prepared by my beautiful soon-to-be wife and her just as beautiful daughter." My father is good.

"Yeah, yeah." Sarah isn't buying it. "So the next day?" She

is relentless.

My father laughs and I know what's coming. "Well my son here decided he wanted to do a little bull riding."

Both women stop eating and look at us.

"You're kidding?" Sarah says wide-eyed.

I shake my head.

"Nope, so we made a little detour through Wyoming and found a ranch just outside of Jackson Hole and this crazy bastard rode a big black bull named Black Death, twice."

Both women are wide-eyed with their mouths even wider.

"Oh my God. That is insane." Jessica says. "Did you actually stay on the thing?"

"Well the first time it bucked me off right away, but the second time I rode it for like four seconds."

"That is crazy." Jessica says.

"Did you get hurt at all?" Sarah asks as a concerned mother would.

"Not really, it bucked me off pretty good both times but I was okay, nothing broken, no blood, just sore bones and muscles and a couple scrapes here and there." My father starts chuckling. "What?" I say.

"Oh nothing...I just got the vision of you flipping over that bull like a trapeze artist." He starts laughing a little louder now and Jessica joins him. Sarah does not think it's funny.

"John, that's not funny, he could have been seriously injured...or even killed."

"But he wasn't and he is sitting here alive and well."

"Yeah I know, but still." Now I know why my father decided not to mention the skydiving thing. She no doubt would have killed him, for not only doing it himself, but for making me do it as well. "So after the bull riding?"

"Well, we headed up to the Tetons, walked around Jenny lake, and then camped out in the campground by the lake. The next day we checked out Old Faithful and then stayed in Butte. Then we came here."

"That sounds like a fun father and son trip." Sarah says.

"It was." I say.

"Yeah, it was great." My father adds.

We finish up our food and my father and I clear the table and wash the dishes as the women drink wine by the fire on the deck out back. After we take care of the dishes we grab a couple beers and join them. We talk for a little while longer about Montana and the wedding and then my father and Sarah head to bed. My father reminds me that we have some fishing to do in the morning and that I shouldn't stay up too late. I stay up an hour longer talking with Jessica, mostly about her, her work, her college experience, and her failed love life. She is a cool chick and I am glad that she is now part of my small family and that I am part of hers. She decides to stay so I give her my room and I sleep on the couch in the living room. I can't wait to hit the Big Blackfoot tomorrow with the old man and do some fly fishing, it should be a great day.

CHAPTER SEVEN

I awake to the smell of coffee and bacon coming from the kitchen. I lie there for several seconds, stretching, rubbing my eyes, trying to wake up. The smells from the kitchen are calling me though and I finally toss the blanket off of me and sit up on the couch. After a few seconds I stand up and head towards the kitchen. When I enter the kitchen my father is in front of the stove cooking bacon. An entire pound of bacon is already cooked and cooling on a plate next to him.

"You think that's enough bacon there old man?"

He turns his head around, looks at me, and smiles. "Hell, this is only half of it." I shake my head. He grabs a coffee mug and extends it towards me. "Coffee?"

"Yes, please." I take the mug from him and head to the refrigerator to grab some milk or hopefully some creamer. After searching for a few seconds I find a bottle of Irish crème creamer and grab it. I pour a couple seconds worth of it into my mug and then place it back in the door of the fridge where I found it. Then I head over to the coffee maker, grab the carafe and fill my mug up the rest of the way with what I am sure is some sort of gourmet coffee. I can't imagine my father or Sarah drinking Maxwell House or Folgers. I grab a spoon and stir the coffee and creamer together into a light brown mixture of deliciousness. I take a drink and it instantly warms my throat, then my belly, and then my soul.

"Bacon?" My father is standing there holding a plate containing a literal six inch high mound of bacon. My mouth begins to water as I take a strip of the greatest food ever created and take a bite. My father grabs a plate and adds several strips of bacon to it and sets it down in front of me. "Enjoy."

"Thanks dad." I say with a mouth full of bacon. I wash it down with another drink of Irish crème coffee.

After I eat several more strips of bacon and drink two more cups of coffee I head to my room. Right before I am about to enter the room I remember that Jessica is in there asleep so I decide to just wear what I am wearing to go fishing in and turn back towards the living room. I hear my father outside so I head out there to see if he needs any help. He is loading the truck up with fishing rods, baskets, nets, and other fishing equipment.

"Need some help?"

He turns and looks at me. "Sure, can you grab the cooler and fill it with some of those Moose Drools we got last night?"

"Okay."

"And throw some ice on it from the freezer."

"Okay." I grab the cooler and head back inside. I fill the cooler with twelve beers and dump some ice over it. I close the cooler and carry it outside. I set it on the truck's tailgate and then slide it into the truck bed, which is now filled with fly fishing gear, including a couple pair of galoshes and two folding chairs.

"You ready?" My father asks as he comes around from the front of the truck to the back.

"I think so."

"Alrighty, let's go catch us some fish."

I go close the front door to the house and then jump in the passenger seat. My father starts the truck, puts it in gear, and heads to the main road, highway 200. He turns right and heads east down the highway. Ten minutes later we take a left onto Johnsrud Park Road and then drive a few minutes before my father pulls over on the side of the road.

"Okay, here we are."

We get out and head to the back of the truck. My father opens the tailgate and grabs the two chairs while I grab the cooler. We walk down to the bank of the Big Blackfoot and set

the chairs and cooler down and then head back to the truck.
My father grabs the rods, the baskets, and a small box that I
assume contains his flies. I grab the nets
and the galoshes and we head back to where we set down the
chairs and cooler.

"Alright son, let's get these chairs set up and relax for a
second while I tie these flies onto our lines." We each grab a
chair, unfold it, and take a seat. My father grabs his rod and
then grabs the small box. "Put those galoshes on." I do what
he says as he opens the box, takes out a fly, and ties it to the
line. He then repeats the same on the rod that I will use. When
he is done he closes and sets the small box down and then
hands me the rod I will be using.

"Okay, you ready to learn how to fly fish?"

"As ready as I'll ever be."

He put his galoshes on and we stand up and head towards
the Big Blackfoot, rods in hand. When we get there the lesson
begins.

"Okay, now this is different than bait cast fishing or so-
called regular fishing. In bait cast fishing you throw the bait
out into the water and then either reel it in or let it sit out there
in the water attached to a bobber. In fly fishing the goal is to
simulate a fly, flying over the water and then gently landing on
the water. You don't want to just splash it down, that will scare
the fish off. Okay?"

"Got it."

"Good, now how do you cast? Well the first thing you need

to know is that the fly is very light, all the weight is actually in the line. So think of the fly line as a lead weight that you're casting out. Now you want to let out several feet of line like this and then you want to hold the rod just above the reel and hold the line with your middle finger like this and then hold the excess line in your other hand like this."

I watch intently as my father demonstrates. "Then what you want to do is you want to flick it back and then forward, quickly at first and then slower as the line goes out. You don't want to go too far back or too far forward, just flick the end of it, and then let a little bit of line slip through your fingers like this. Now you don't have to cast way out there, just about ten to twenty feet. I know when most people bait fish they like to throw that rod back and then heave that bait as far as they can, but that's not necessary here. Just flick it back and forth at a slight forty-five degree angle, as close to the water without touching it. Then you shoot the line and try to set the fly down on top of the water as gently as possible."

I continue to watch intently as he demonstrates. "Now, when you set the fly on the water you want to tighten the line so you can feel when you get a fish on so you lower the rod so it is basically pointing at the fly and then you do what we call strip away, which is you pull the line with your off hand through the middle finger of your rod hand like this. Now when that fish bites you squeeze that middle finger and then raise the rod like this. Hopefully that fly will hook the fish and then you reel him in. Now, when you reel the fish in you want to take your time. It shouldn't be a first round knockout; it should be a twelve round unanimous decision in your favor of course. Wear that fish out and when you get him close to the bank you use the net to grab him and then you toss him in your basket and that's it."

"Oh is that it?" I say sarcastically.

"Just remember, flick, shoot, strip, hook, reel."

"Okay, I think I can remember that."

"Well, watch me cast a few times and take some mental notes and then when you're ready just head up river and give it a shot."

"Okay."

I watch my father cast out several times, but I only watch his technique for the first three times. The other times I find myself just watching him. A week ago I had no idea who he was and now I'm standing here on a bank of the Big Blackfoot River in the middle of Montana watching him fly fish. Watching him doing something that he only came to love because of a book I just happened to buy him ten years ago. And at that moment I realize that if I had never bought him that book he would never have come up here to fly fish. He would have never met Jim and in turn he would have never met Sarah. And he more than likely wouldn't be getting married tomorrow and we wouldn't be here together or anywhere for that matter. The insanity of that thought blows my mind.

"You gonna fish or what?" My father says to me, breaking

my brain cloud.

"Yeah." I turn and head up river, the crazy thought still swimming around in my head, I hope I can concentrate on this fishing business and hook at least one.

When I get to the spot I decide to fish, I look around and drink in the awesomeness before me. My father told me on the drive from Butte that the Big Blackfoot is a majestic, spiritual river that originates at the continental divide and runs west through western Montana. He said the river valley is surrounded by mountains and rolling hills that were formed by receding glaciers at the end of the last ice age. He also mentioned that Douglas firs, spruces, and cottonwood trees shoot up out of the rocky soil towards the big blue sky shading parts of the Big Blackfoot. He told me that the river is loaded with rainbow, brown, and brook trout, among others.

As I stand there and soak in the scenery, I can now see with my own eyes what he described to me a couple of days ago. I inhale the clean mountain air until my lungs are full and then exhale, slowly, closing my eyes. I open them and look over at my father who is whipping that fly rod like a pro, back and forth, back and forth, and it is beautiful.

I decide to give this fly fishing thing a shot and I take a few steps into the river's water. I do as my father had taught me, I let out some line and start flicking the rod back and forth, quickly at first and then I get into a somewhat melodic flow with it. I follow the line with my eyes, turning my head to follow it behind me and then turning it back as it flies forward. I am in a trance and forget to shoot it onto the water. I am just going back and forth with it like a machine.

"Hey, are you gonna actually drop that fly or just fly it around all day?" My father yells, breaking my trance.

I stop my cast and my line falls making my fly get caught up in some tall grasses.

"Hey, I'm practicing. You just worry about catching some fish old man." I say with a smile and he smile back.

I start the flicking up again and once again get into a melodic flow with it. When I feel ready I shoot the line and the fly forward and land it on the clear icy water. I strip the line, tightening it, slowly moving the fly over the water's surface until it disappears. I tighten my finger on the line and pull the rod up hooking that little bastard. The fish on the end of my line fights like a champ and I remember my father's words, "It's not a first round knockout, it's a twelve round decision," and I ease up on the line but not too much.

"Fish on. Fish on." I yell and my father turns his head and looks at me.

"That a kid, don't lose him."

I figure he would run over and help me reel it in, but no such luck, this is my fish from beginning to end, and I am glad he didn't come over and help.

I reel it in slowly, let some line out here and there. The fish is slowly getting closer to me and after a good five minutes the fish is exhausted from the fight and basically gives up. I reel it right up to the bank, grab my net and lift it out of the icy waters of the Big Blackfoot. I take a few steps away from the river bank and then set the rod and the net down. The fish, still in the net, is a beautiful rainbow trout that is a couple inches over a foot long and probably weighs anywhere from three to four pounds. As I remove the fly from its mouth, my father walks up to check it out.

"Nice fish son. And on your first cast. I guess it's true, anyone can be a fisherman in May."

"What's that mean?"

"Oh nothing, it's just an old Hemingway quote."

"Yeah, well I had a pretty good teacher." I grab the fish and stand up, holding it like a trophy.

My father smiles. "Alright ya big show off, toss him in the basket and we'll take him home with us."

I smile and do as he says. We fish for about an hour before we take a break and a seat in our folding chairs. We sit there in silence enjoying our natural surroundings and a couple of Moose Drools.

"Do you believe in God?" I say out of the blue and break the silence.

My father looks at me and then looks back at the Big Blackfoot. "I believe in something, maybe not an old bearded guy up in the clouds, but something. I mean what is God? What does that mean? Is it a person? Is it a celestial being? Is it some sort of cosmic life force? I don't know son. All I know is that I've made some mistakes in my life and I wish I could take most of them back, but I'm a good person and if there is a

God I think he or she or it will know that and I'll be given peace in death."

"Are you afraid of death, of dying?"

He looks at me again and then looks back at the Big Blackfoot. "I think everyone is afraid of dying, but you can't live your life in fear of death or you will never truly live. Death comes for everyone at some point. The trick is to avoid him for as long as you can. You can be afraid of dying, but when it comes, you just have to accept it, which I've done."

I take a drink of my beer and think about what he just said. "It's not fair." I finally say.

"What's not fair?"

"It's not fair that we come back into each other's lives and that this fucking cancer is going to take you away from me again."

"Yeah, well life's not fair son. It is what it is."

"Well it's bullshit. I wish I could do something. I feel so helpless."

My father takes a drink of his beer and I follow his lead. "It is a helpless situation son, but you know what?"

"What?"

"We've had this week, we've had this day, we have right now, and we have tomorrow. And even though that's not a lot of time, it's better than no time at all." He looks at me and I look and him. He extends his bottle of Moose Drool towards me and I clank my bottle against his and we both take a drink of our respective beers. And he's right, we have had a great time reconnecting this week and we still have a wedding tomorrow and maybe even some more fishing on Sunday, who knows. I love my father, I always have, and I always will. And as I think about him tears slide down my cheeks.

He stares out towards the Big Blackfoot and the mountains and trees beyond it not noticing my grief. I turn and look out over that majestic flowing body of water and I thank God, whatever that is, for this moment and for every moment before and after this. And I am thankful to be alive and to be here with my father, fishing, talking, drinking, and just being.

We sit there for a while longer on the bank of the Big Blackfoot, drinking beer and relaxing in the warm afternoon Montana sunshine. We fish for another hour and I catch nothing, my father catches two rainbows and one brown trout.

"We better head back to the house. We have a wedding dinner in a couple of hours." My father yells.

"Okay." I yell back.

I grab all my fishing gear and make my way back over to where my father is. We load up our fishing gear into the truck and then go back for the chairs and cooler. We load that into the back of the truck, jump in, and then head back to highway 200. We head west down highway 200 and arrive back at the house soon after. We unload the truck and then head to the back deck to gut and clean the four fish we caught. My father handles his fillet knife like a surgeon handles his or her scalpel and the four fish are ready for the freezer in minutes. After we clean up all the fish guts and heads and fins, we head inside to shower and get ready for the big wedding dinner, which will be held at the Big Sky Brewery Tap Room in about an hour and a half.

After I shower and get dressed I head to the kitchen. My father and Sarah are standing by the island enjoying a drink and each other's company. They turn and look at me as I walk in.

"Hey son."

"Mr. and Mrs. Bennett." I say with a chuckle. They both smile.

"Not yet, Son." He looks at Sarah and she looks at him. "But not soon enough." They both smile at one another and kiss and I smile. "Grab a beer son, we'll leave in fifteen minutes."

"Cool." I walk over to the refrigerator, open it, and pull out a bottle of Moose Drool. I grab the bottle opener from the drawer, open my beer, and take a drink. "So, who's all going to be there tonight?" I ask both of them.

"Well, the entire wedding party. The three of us, Jessica, Jim, Sarah's parents, David, and our other friends Holly, Tim, Nadine, and Paul." My father takes a drink of his beer and I follow suit.

"That's it?"

"That's it." My father answers.

"We didn't want a big wedding, just family and close friends." Sarah adds.

"And where is the ceremony gonna be again?"

"It's gonna be right outside behind the house on the bank of the Big Blackfoot."

"Oh yeah, that's right, you told me that already."

"Yep. We love that river. It's where we fell in love and where we spend most of our free time. I can't think of any other place to marry this woman." They kiss again and I smile again. I am so happy that my father found Sarah and that she found him.

"Alright, enough with this sappy stuff, we have to get going." Sarah insists.

When we get to the Big Sky Brewery Tap Room everyone is there already, except for Jessica who is apparently running late. Sarah takes a seat and orders us some beers while my father introduces me to everyone.

"Everyone, this is my son Andrew, Andrew, this is everyone." My father, the gentleman. Everyone says hi in synchronicity and I say hi to everyone back. We take a seat as our beers arrive and we wait for Jessica before ordering food. Jessica finally shows up with some guy.

"Hey Jessica, there you are." My father says. "Who's your friend?"

Jessica looks at the guy next to her and then looks back at us. "Mom. John. This is Brian." She points at Brian. "Brian, this is my mom and my soon to be step-father John." She points at them.

He shakes their hands. "Nice to meet both of you." Brian says with a smile.

"It's nice to meet you too Brian." Sarah says smiling back.

"And this is my soon to be step-brother Andrew." We shake hands and repeat the nice to meet you mantra. "And this is everyone else." She extends her arm towards the table. "Everyone, this is my friend Brian." They all say hello and give a quick wave. Jessica and Brian take the final two seats at the table and order a couple of beers. The thirteen of us each take turns ordering food as the waitress circles the table franticly taking down everyone's orders.

While the food is being prepared my father stands up and clinks his pint glass with his fork. "If I could have everyone's attention please I would like to say a few words." Everyone stops talking and looks at my father. "First of all I want to thank all of you for coming tonight and for coming tomorrow. We can't wait to share our special day with all of you. Next, I would like to thank my son, for not only agreeing to accompany me on my trip up from Flagstaff or for agreeing to be my best man, but for making all of this possible. You see, ten years ago my son bought me a book. A little book about family and fly fishing set right here in the great town of Missoula, Montana. A book called *A River Runs Through It*.

Now I know most of you already know this story, but I'm gonna tell it again anyway. So a couple years later I finally picked up that book and read it and then I found out there was a film and I watched it and then I said to myself, self, we're gonna go up to Montana and we're gonna learn how to fly fish. And I packed up the old truck and a drove a thousand miles straight north. And then I met Jim and then I met Sarah and the rest as they say is history." He looks at me as he raises his glass. Everyone raises their glasses too, as do I. "Thank you son."

I smile and nod my head and we all take a drink of our beers. "Next, I want to thank Jim for being my wingman on that fateful night and for being my best friend these past eight years." Jim nods.

"And finally, I want to thank Sarah." He looks at her and she looks at him. "I want to thank you for everything. For letting me into your life. For loving me unconditionally. For wanting to marry me. And of course for being by my side during all this...stuff." I had almost forgotten about my father's cancer until he said that. But I brush that thought away like a pesky fly not wanting to think about it. They kiss and we all raise our glasses again and take another drink. I feel like I have to say something being the best man and all so I stand up and everyone looks at me.

"I just have a few things to say real quick. Um..." I try to find the words since I didn't have anything prepared. "I just want to say that I'm happy for both of you and that I'm glad that I could be a part of this special occasion." I look directly at my father. "And Dad, I want to thank you for making me your best man and basically forcing me to drive up from Flagstaff with you." Everyone chuckles a little bit. "And even though I was scared shitless, thank you for fulfilling my dream of riding a bull and convincing me to jump out of a plane with you." No one chuckles, not even a little bit. Sarah looks at my father as does everyone else.

"Hold on, what was that? Who jumped out of a plane? John?" Her voice rises a bit.

My father looks at me like thanks for letting the cat out of the bag. "What?" he finally says.

"Did you take your son skydiving?" Did you jump out of a plane?" Her voice is raised a bit more.

He looks at her. "Sort of."

"Sort of? What does that mean? How do you sort of jump out of a plane?"

"Well, the instructor was the one who actually jumped out of the plane, I was just attached to him." My father explains as he forms a big cheesy grin on his face.

Sarah shakes her head. "I can't believe you." Her slight frown turns into a slight smile. "Ugh, you are so frustrating sometimes." She gives him a kiss on the lips. "You are so lucky that I'm crazy in love with you."

"I'm the luckiest guy in the world that's for sure." My father smiles and then kisses Sarah on the lips again. I decide to end my speech on that note and I sit back down.

At that moment the food begins to arrive one by one and we eat and we drink and then we dance. I spend a little time on the make shift dance floor that is really just the floor with tables and chairs moved out of the way. But I spend most of the time watching my father and Sarah. Watching them slow dance. Watching them smile at each other. Watching them kiss.

And watching them immersed in each other's existence. They were in love, real, true, passionate love and I was proud to have a part in it and I was thankful for the opportunity to witness it.

The night continued on back at the house with most of the wedding party making the drive, with only David, who was to perform the ceremony, not joining us. We drank some more and ate some more and danced some more and it was electric and warm and perfect. People left the house and headed home here and there and then at about a quarter to midnight Jessica and her friend Brian left, leaving only myself, my father, and Sarah in the house.

We talk for a few minutes but realize quickly how late it is and decide to call it a night. My father and Sarah head to their room as I start to clean up the kitchen a bit. I gather all of the garbage and toss it into the trash can. Then I gather all of the dirty glasses and small plates, rinse them off and out, and load them into the dishwasher. I finish up by putting away all the left out food and by wiping down all of the countertops. I head to my room and get into my sleeping attire, which is just a t-shirt and a pair of boxer shorts. I hop into bed and peer out through the window blinds and look at the almost full moon as it sits there, motionless, in the dark sky above. And before I fall asleep I playback the past five days in my head and I smile at first, but then I begin to cry.

CHAPTER EIGHT

I awake to no alarm, no smells of breakfast coming from
the kitchen, no knocks on my bedroom door, nothing, I just
wake up for no reason at all. Maybe it was the fact that today
is the wedding and I am excited or nervous or some other
feeling. As I lie in bed staring at the ceiling the vision of
Raelynn, the waitress at the Denny's in Flagstaff, appears in
my head for some reason. I picture her big, beautiful southern
smile and her big green eyes and it makes me smile. Then the
vision of my father and I fishing replaces Raelynn's smiling
face.

I remember watching him fish, a man in total
concentration with one thing on his mind, not the cancer, not

the wedding, but just catching a fish. The memory makes me smile again. I look over at the digital alarm clock and it's nine in the morning. I think about trying to fall back asleep, but I decide to get up and prepare for the long day ahead. I throw the covers off of me and slowly slide out of bed. The floor is colder than it has been and it makes me sit back down on the bed. I put on the socks that I wore the day before, grab some clean clothes and head to the door. When I open it my father is standing there about to knock on my door and it startles me.

"Shit dad, you scared the hell out of me."

"Sorry son, good timing though."

"Yeah I guess."

"So I was just coming to tell you that there are donuts in the kitchen and coffee brewing as we speak."

"Okay, cool, I gonna jump in the shower real quick and then I'll head in there."

"Okay."

My father walks down the hall to his bedroom and I head to the guest bathroom. I turn the shower on, undress, and hop in. The water is super warm and steam begins to fill the tiny bathroom. I let the water massage my back and shoulders and then turn around and let it attack the top of my head. Water violently flows over my face as well as my entire body and I am completely relaxed and warm, like I'm back in bed under the heavy down comforter.

After what seems like an hour, but is really ten minutes, I turn the water off and grab my towel. I dry off and then put on my nice clean clothes, which is just, underwear, socks, a pair of jeans and a t-shirt. The mirror is fogged over so I wipe it with the hand towel that is hanging on the towel bar next to the sink. I look at myself in the mirror, examining my face, my chin, my cheeks, my lips, my nose, my eyes, and my forehead, for no apparent reason. I put on some deodorant, grab my dirty clothes, and then head back to my room. I toss my dirties onto the floor in the corner with my other dirties and then head to the kitchen.

There is a pink box on the island that I assume contains donuts and a pot of coffee in the coffee maker. My father and Sarah are nowhere to be found. I grab a mug and fill it with coffee and some Irish crème creamer. Then I walk over and open the pink box, which not surprisingly contains donuts. I take a maple long john from the box, take a bite, and then I wash it down with some coffee. At that moment my father walks into the kitchen.

"How is it?" he asks.

"How is what?"

"The maple bar."

"Oh, it tastes like it always does, delicious."

"Good." My father grabs a mug and fills it with coffee.

I take another bite of my donut. "It's a maple long john by the way." I say smiling. He turns and looks at me.

"It is what it is."

I look at him like he just said something that didn't make any sense. "What does that mean?"

He laughs. "I don't know, it just popped in my head so I said it."

I laugh with him. "So where's Sarah?"

"She's with Jessica. They're getting the final wedding arrangements taken care of."

"Cool, so what's the plan today?" I take another bite of my maple long john as my father reaches into the box and takes a chocolate donut with nuts on it.

"Well, they are doing what I just said and we are just relaxing."

"We are?"

"Yes sir, I thought we would take some chairs and a cooler down to the Big Blackfoot and just sit and drink and enjoy the river's mystic existence."

"Shit, that sounds good to me. What time is the wedding?"

"The ceremony is at five and the reception is here at the house right after."

"Alright, so we have seven hours of relaxing to accomplish, awesome."

"Yep, oh and Jim is gonna join us around noon, he's gonna bring us some lunch and relax with us until the wedding."

"Nice, I haven't got a chance to talk with him that much."

"Well you will, he is a great guy."

I finish my donut and grab another one, a chocolate long john this time. Then I walk over and refill my mug, with coffee and some more Irish crème creamer. My father disappears for thirty minutes as I continue to scarf down half of the donuts in the box and almost an entire pot of coffee. He appears out of nowhere with a case of Moose Drool in his arms.

"Son, can you grab the two bags of ice from the truck while I grab the cooler?"

"I can." I head to the truck, grab the two seven pound bags of store bought ice, and return to the kitchen. My father walks in shortly after holding the cooler, which he sets on the kitchen floor. He starts to add bottles of Moose Drool to the cooler.

"Alright, let's get a layer of ice on these beers." I walk over and slam the bag of ice on the floor to break it up. Then I tear open the bag and pour its entire contents onto the sixteen beers that are now calling this cooler home. My father throws the other eight beers into the refrigerator and the other bag of ice into the freezer. I close the lid of the cooler and for some reason I ask myself if the darkness will scare my new cold little friends.

"Can you carry that yourself?"

I lift it up. "Yeah I can manage."

"Okay, I'll grab the chairs and meet you out back."

I head out the back sliding glass door as my father heads to the truck to get the chairs. We meet in the back and walk down to the bank of the Big Blackfoot. I set the cooler down and open one of the chairs as my father opens the other one. We sit down, the cooler between us, and we stare out at the Big Blackfoot and beyond it at the beautiful Montana landscape.

"Beer me son." My father finally says. I open the cooler,

grab two bottles of Moose Drool, and close the lid. I set both of the beers on top of the cooler as my father gets the bottle opener from his pants pocket. He opens both bottles and we both take one in our hand and take a drink.

"So, what does the future hold for you son?"

"The future? I have no idea."

"No plans? What about school? You gonna finish?"

"I don't think so, hell I don't know, maybe."

"You want some advice?" We both take another swig of our beers.

"Sure."

"Do what's gonna make you happy son. If it's finishing your degree then do it. If it's not finishing then don't. Life is too damn short not to do what makes you happy. It shouldn't take your impending death to figure that out, but that is when most people do. When we're young we don't realize that it could all be over just like that. You should know that better than others. You can't go through life scared to make the tough decisions. So many people are stuck in jobs they hate, but they are scared to quit, scared to change careers, scared of starting over, scared of being broke and homeless. And then there's love. People are scared of rejection so they never ask out that girl they like and they might just miss out on the greatest thing this world has to offer us."

"And what's that?"

"Love son. Shit, without love life is meaningless. It's love that makes us wake up every morning. It's love that makes us fall asleep with a smile on our face every night. It's love that makes life worth living. And it's not just romantic love. It's loving your work, it's loving where you live and what you do for fun. It's loving life, all aspects of it."

"You sound like Bill."

"Who's Bill?"

"He's that guy that gave me a ride to Flagstaff, the guy that dropped me off at the Denny's."

"Well, he's a pretty smart guy." We both take another swig of our beers.

"Well, I love where I live and I sort of love my work. I mean I don't hate it, it is work. So I guess that just leaves the romantic love left."

"Well, like I told you before, that will come, it always does, you just have to be patient, but not too patient. Promise me you'll go after the girl son."

"What girl?"

"The girl. The one who will change your life. The one you may or may not have even met yet." I think of Emily at that moment and then she fades from my mind and is replaced by Raelynn's smiling face.

"I promise old man. If I meet the one, I will get her number no matter what it takes."

"That a boy." We both finish off our beers at the same time and I grab us another. Thirty minutes and two beers later we hear someone walking behind us and we both turn to see who or what it is.

"You boys start the party without me?" Jim says. He is carrying a big brown paper bag in his hands.

"We sure did ya old bastard." My father repies. "Is that lunch?" my father asks.

"Yes it is, three pulled pork and brisket sandwiches and three sides of barbeque beans."

My mouth instantly waters. I give Jim my chair and run up to the garage to grab another one for myself.

When I return the food is out of the bag and on top of the cooler. I set my chair up in front of the cooler in-between my father and Jim. I grab a sandwich, unwrap it, and take a bite. My father does the same as Jim starts in on his side of barbeque beans.

"So what you guys chattin' about down here?" Jim asks.

"Oh the usual, life and love." My father answers.

"Oh hell John, you givin' the boy the love everything speech?"

I laugh.

"Of course, it's a good speech."

Jim chuckles. "Yeah, I guess it is."

We continue to attack our delicious lunch.

"So Jim, do you love your work?" I ask.

His mouth is full of barbeque bean and he waits until he finishes that bite before he answers. "Yes I do."

"And what is it that you do?"

"I own a fly fishing shop."

"No shit?"

"No shit. I used to be in the insurance business but I hated it. So when I was forty-five I quit my job, got a business loan from the bank, and opened up my shop. I used my saving to buy my first bit of inventory and the rest, as they say, is history."

"That's awesome Jim."

"See son, it's never too late to do what you love."

Jim nods his head in agreement.

We spend the next couple of hour finishing up our lunch, drinking beers, and telling stories. My father tells the story again of how he and Sarah met. Jim fills in the gaps and corrects the events that my father exaggerated. Jim tells a story about the time he hooked a ten pound brown trout, which my father argued was only eight pounds. They went back and forth on the subject for a good ten minutes. I suggest that they agree on nine pounds and they both reject that suggestion. I tell the story of Max, Bear and I's trip up to Seattle a couple years ago. How we picked up Crazy J and messed with him by pulling a fake grab and run. How we partied in Chico and Seattle and how Max met Caroline and the love story that followed. My father liked that story and said that I will find my Caroline soon enough. My father, the romantic.

At three-thirty we decided to head back up to the house and get ready for the wedding. As we make our way up towards the house from the Big Blackfoot Sarah appears on the back deck.

"You guys better not be drunk." She yells.

We all laugh.

"We're as sober as a priest on a Saturday night sweetheart."

She glared at us. "Well I'm not sure how sober that is."

We all laugh again. When we get to the top of the deck my father and Sarah embrace and then kiss.

"You ready to be my wife?"

"I don't know are you ready to be my husband?"

"I've been ready since the first time I laid my eyes on you." My father, the romantic.

"You're good, real good." She says smiling. They kiss again. Sarah gives Jim a hug after he sets the chairs down and then she gives me one after I set the cooler down. We all head inside.

Things happen quickly over the next hour. People come and go setting things up down by the river for the wedding and inside the house and on the deck for the reception. I try to help out, but Sarah tells me there is no need, so I grab a beer and chill out in the living room where no one is doing anything. I turn on the television and watch the end of the University of Montana versus Boise State baseball game that is already in the eighth inning. At four-thirty Jessica comes into the living room and tells me it's time to get ready so I turn off the television and head to my room to get my nice shirt and tie on.

My father told me a couple days ago that we are just wearing jeans with our nice shirts and ties to the wedding. When I later protested that idea he told me it doesn't matter what we wear, what matters is that he gets to marry the most amazing woman in the world. He said he would marry her in his boxer shorts if that's all he had. I laugh at the memory of that conversation.

When I'm finally dressed I head outside to the back deck, where I see Jessica standing with Brian, her guy friend from last night's dinner.

"Is everything set?" I ask.

She turns her head, looks at me, and smiles. She is wearing a beautiful peach colored dress with spaghetti straps. The dress barely covers her knees and she looks incredible. Brian is in basically the same get up as I am, just with a different color shirt and tie.

"Yep, everyone is taking their seats. My mother is in her room with my grandfather and your father…" She pauses and looks behind me. "…is right there."

I turn just as my father steps onto the deck.

"Alright, let's get this show on the road." My father says. He is wearing a white dress shirt with a single white rose corsage pinned to it. His tie is striped in white and grey. He is also decked out in a nice pair of jeans, and a nice pair of black cowboy boots. He hands me the ring and I put it in my pocket.

The three of us head down to the river bank and take our places. David, the guy performing the wedding is standing with the Big Blackfoot right behind him. My father stands in front of him just off to his left side and I stand right next to him. Jessica stands on the other side of David, leaving a place for her mother. In front of us are eight white folding chairs all occupied except for two. One of which is for Sarah's father after he walks her down the aisle and gives her away. The other is for Sarah's friend Nadine who is now standing behind the chairs holding a mandolin.

At five past five Sarah and her father appear on the back deck and everyone stands up. As they make their way down to us Nadine begins to play the wedding march on her mandolin. Her father is wearing a white dress shirt with a bolo tie, a nice pair of jeans, and an old pair of black cowboy boots. Sarah is wearing a simple white dress with spaghetti straps that falls just past her knees. She is holding a bouquet of white roses and has a huge smile on her face. I turn and look at my father and he is smiling just as big, watching her walk down towards him. When they finally make their way to us, David begins the ceremony.

"Everyone may be seated." Those that are supposed to sit do so. "We are here to celebrate love. More specifically, the love between these two dear friends of mine, John Bennett and Sarah Campbell. Now, since I know everyone that is here and I know that everyone wants these two to be married I will just skip that silly part." Everyone laughs. "So who gives this woman to this man?"

"Her mother and I do." Sarah's father says. He then walks her to my father's side. They shake hands and then he sits down next to his wife.

My father grabs Sarah's hands and David continues. "Now

I was instructed, strike that, I was forced to make this as quick as possible so here we go." We all laugh again. "John Bennett do you promise to be faithful to Sarah? To take care of her when she is ill? To start every day with her and end every night with her? To take her fly fishing once in a while?" Everyone laughs again causing David to pause. "John do you promise to love Sarah for all eternity?"

"I promise." My father says with a smile.

"Sarah Campbell do you promise to be faithful to John? To take care of him when he is ill?" At that, a single tear slides down her face. "To start every day with him and end every night with him? To let him go fly fishing by himself or with just his friends once in a while?" Everyone laughs again causing David to pause again. "Sarah do you promise to love John for all eternity?"

"I promise." She says as she smiles and wipes the tear from her cheek.

"Okay, now we need the rings." David says.

I reach into my pocket, pull out the ring, and hand it to my father. Jessica does the same and hands it to her mother.

David continues. "John, please place the ring on Sarah's left ring finger and repeat after me." He slides the ring on her finger and holds it. "This ring is just a symbol of my love for you."

"This ring is just a symbol of my love for you."

"If I should happen to lose it while fishing."

Everyone laughs again causing David to pause again.

"If I should happen to lose it while fishing."

"Know that my eternal love for you will always be in my heart."

"Know that my eternal love for you will always be in my heart."

"Now Sarah, please place the ring on John's left ring finger and repeat after me." She slides the ring on my father's finger and holds it. "This ring is not just a symbol of my love for you."

"This ring is not just a symbol of my love for you."

"If you lose it while fishing I will kill you."

Everyone laughs causing David to pause once again.

"If you lose it while fishing I will kill you."

"But know that my eternal love for you will always be in my heart."

"But know that my eternal love for you will always be in my heart."

"Now by the power vested in me by the great state of Montana, I now pronounce you husband and wife, John you may kiss your new bride." They kiss and everyone stands and cheers. They turn and face everyone. "Ladies and gentlemen, let me introduce to you for the first time, Mr. and Mrs. John Bennett." Everyone continues to stand and cheer. "Now let's party." David yells.

Sarah's friend plays an exit song on the mandolin as my father and new step-mother walk back towards the house together as husband and wife. Jessica walks over to me and gives me a side hug.

"This is the best day of my life." I say to her.

"Mine too." She says back.

We take our turn walking down the aisle and everyone else follows us. We all head to the back deck and get the reception started.

The reception is fun, just like the wedding. My father and Sarah dance their first dance as a married couple to Mazzy Star's *Fade Into You,* which was the first song they had ever danced to. We all drink way too much and eat way too much, but it is a great time, the perfect ending to a perfect day and in reality a perfect week. The thought of my father's cancer never once entered my head that is until I went to bed. As I lie there I replay the entire ceremony in my head and I remember that tear that slid down Sarah's cheek. And I remember why and tears start to slide down my cheeks.

CHAPTER NINE

I am jolted awake by a horrible nightmare. My father and I were fishing at the spot we were at a couple of days ago and he hooked a huge fish that he fought for a good twenty minutes. He finally managed to reel the massive fish close to the bank and when he went to grab it, it jumped out of the Big Blackfoot and swallowed his entire arm all the way to the shoulder. He was completely surprised and caught off guard by the attack. He lost his balance, fell into the clear, icy water, and disappeared. I dove into the Big Blackfoot to save him but he was nowhere to be seen.

As the icy river water carried me downstream I continued to dive down to locate him but to no avail. I noticed the river disappearing ahead and I attempted to swim back upstream but the water was too powerful and I eventually succumb to its rage. I fell over what I assumed was a waterfall and then I was jolted awake as I fell into a dark endless abyss.

I lie in bed sweating, trying to calm my rapidly beating heart, which I do after a good ten minutes. I look over at the digital alarm clock at it reads four fifteen in the morning. I close my eyes and try to fall back asleep.

I am awoken again, this time not by a nightmare, but by a gentle knock on the bedroom door. I don't respond and then I hear the door open slowly.

"Andrew." It's a woman's voice, Sarah's voice.

"Yeah." I respond as I rub my eyes.

"Can I come in?" She pokes her head in.

"Yeah, of course." I stretch my entire body as she walks in. She stops at the foot of the bed and stares at me with no expression on her face. I look at her and notice that she looks like she has been crying. "What's going on?" I sit up in bed. Sarah puts her left hand over her nose and mouth and looks away. She looks back at me and then removes her hand from her face. Tears slide down both of her cheeks. "Sarah, what's wrong? What's going on?" She takes a deep breath, and exhales.

"Your father didn't wake up this morning. He's gone." Her words do not resonate with me.

"What? What do you mean gone?" I say, even though I know deep down what has happened.

"Andrew, your father has passed away, he's dead." She starts crying harder now and covers her face with both of her hands. Her words stab my heart like an arrow as I lie there not knowing what to do or say. I finally realize what is happening and I get out of bed. I walk over to her and give her a hug. She embraces me as she continues to cry, now into my right shoulder. Tears begin to well up and slide down both of my cheeks. We stand there for several minutes holding each other, crying into each other's shoulders. We finally release our hold on each other and wipe away our tears.

"So what do we do now?" I ask.

"I don't know. I guess I should call 911 or the hospital or...I don't know. I didn't expect this to happen this soon." She puts her hands over her face again as she begins to cry again. She leans forward and rests her head on my chest.

"Why don't you call Jessica and I'll call 911, I'm sure they will know what to do or who to send." She leans back, off my chest and wipes her eyes.

"Okay." She says and I take a deep breath and exhale. I walk over and grab my cellphone. "You should probably use the house phone so they know the address."

"Good idea." I set my cellphone back down and leave the bedroom. I feel Sarah follow me out but she heads down the hall as I make my way to the kitchen where the house phone is. I pick up the phone receiver and push the 9 button, then the 1 button, and then the 1 button again. I can hear the line ring on the other end and I wait. Someone finally answers.

"911, what is your emergency?" The female dispatcher on the other end of the line says to me.

"Well, I'm not really sure. My father didn't wake up this morning. He has cancer and we think he passed away in his sleep."

"Okay, well I'm sorry to hear that sir. I will send an ambulance and they will handle it from there, okay?"

"Okay, thank you." I hang up the phone before she can respond. I stand there not knowing what to do next. I don't know if I want to go and see my father or try to find Sarah or what, so I just stand there and wait. Sarah walks into the kitchen just as she is saying goodbye to Jessica. She presses the end call button on her cellphone and looks at me. Her eyes are red and swollen.

"So, what's the verdict?" she asks.

"They're sending an ambulance. They'll take it from there."

"Okay."

We stand there both not knowing what to do.

"Do you want some coffee? I can make some." I ask.

She takes a few seconds to respond as she stares at the kitchen counter for no apparent reason. "Yeah, I could use some coffee." She looks at me. "But let me make it, I need the distraction."

"Okay, I'll go wait outside for the ambulance. Is Jessica on her way over?"

"Yeah, she should be here soon."

"Okay." I head outside as Sarah grabs the coffee beans from the pantry.

I have no idea what time it is, but when I get outside it feels like about eight in the morning. I turn and look towards the front of the house, to the east. The sun has risen but it's still low in the sky and there is a light foggy haze coming off of the Big Blackfoot, which I can see beyond the house. I turn back around and I see my father's truck in the driveway and I stare at it. The silence out here is eerie. I can't hear a thing, not the running river behind the house, not the wind blowing through the trees, not even a single bird chirping or an insect singing, nothing.

Then the silence is broken by the sound of a vehicle approaching. I turn my head and see a white and red ambulance coming down the road and I follow it with my eyes as it turns into the driveway. It was like that moment every time you see an ambulance coming and you wonder if it's coming to where you are and if it is why and when it doesn't you breathe a sigh of relief. But this time I knew the ambulance was coming here and I already knew why.

The ambulance stops a few feet from me and two paramedics get out, one is a woman around my age, and the other is a man in his early forties. I tell them that my father has cancer and that he is in bed and that he apparently did not wake up. I told them that my step-mother realized it this morning but that I had not seen him yet. I tell them to follow me and I lead them inside the house. Sarah hears us and enters the living room. She takes them to the bedroom while I head to the kitchen to make a cup of coffee. She returns to the kitchen and grabs the cup of coffee off of the island that she had already poured.

"They confirmed it." She says and I nod my head as tears begin to well up in her eyes again. At that moment the front door opens and Jessica runs in and gives her mother a huge hug and they both begin to cry.

"I'm so sorry mom, I'm so sorry." After what feels like five minutes they end their embrace and Jessica looks over at me. She walks over and gives me a hug and tears slide down my cheeks. She pulls away after several seconds and looks at me. "Are you okay?"

I look at her. "Yeah, I'm doin' okay."

"So what do we do now?" Jessica asks us.

I look over at Sarah and she looks at me.

"I don't know, I guess they'll take him somewhere, to the hospital or to the mortuary or wherever." Sarah says.

"We should probably call the mortuary." I suggest.

"I will take care of it." Jessica offers.

"Thanks." I say.

She heads to the living room to make the call. Sarah and I stay in the kitchen and sip on our coffees, still in shock from the events of the morning. As we stand there in silence I think about Sarah and what the future holds for her. Yeah I lost my father, but I get to go back to L.A. and live the rest of my life. She lost her husband, her friend, her lover, the person that she was supposed to wake up next to for the rest of her life. And now she is all alone and my heart aches for her.

The female paramedic walks into the kitchen and Jessica walks in right behind her. "We have him ready to go. We'll take him to the hospital and then the mortuary can get him from there."

"Okay." I say. The paramedic walks out of the kitchen and about a minute later we hear them wheeling my father's body through the house and out the door. "What did the mortuary say?" I ask Jessica.

"They said what she said. They'll pick his body up from the hospital and take care of it from there. They said they already know what to do so there's not much really for us to do."

"So what's the plan? He never mentioned it to me." I ask and Sarah answers.

"He wanted to be cremated and tossed into the Big Blackfoot." I give a half smile and nod my head. I had already figured that is what he had planned. "And he made a tape."

"A tape?"

"Yeah, before he went down to Flagstaff this last time he made a videotape. I haven't seen it, but he said it's kind of like a video will or something. And he also made a CD of music he wanted to be played at the party."

"The party?"

"Yeah, he wants us to throw him a party out on the back deck. He told me he wants us to toss his ashes into the Big

Blackfoot and then have a barbeque on the deck." She cracks her first smile since last night. "And he wants everyone to get drunk and tell their favorite stories or memories about him." Jessica and I both crack tiny smiles. "That was his wish. He told me to play the tape, toss the ashes, and party. He said he didn't want us to mourn his death, but to celebrate his life." She takes a drink of her coffee. "So that is what we are going to do. I need to call Jim."

She leaves the kitchen and heads to her bedroom to grab her phone, even though it is in her pocket. She calls Jim and returns several minutes later. Jessica and I are still in the kitchen drinking coffee.

"So who wants flapjacks?" Sarah asks as she enters the kitchen. "I need to cook something to get my mind off of this right now." Now I know why he called them flapjacks.

"I'll take a stack." I say, even though I am not really that hungry.

"Me too." Jessica adds.

Two and a half days later everyone that was at the wedding, minus Brian, is now in my father and Sarah's living room huddled around the television. Sarah walks over and places a VHS tape into the VCR. I haven't seen one of those in a decade. She sits down on the coach in-between Jessica and myself and hits the play button on the remote control. My father appears on the screen and some of us smile while others tear up, it all depends on where you are in the grieving process. Then he begins to talk.

"Well, if you're all watching this then I am either dead or you cheated and watched it when you weren't supposed to. I'm going to assume that you wouldn't sneak a peek and that the cancer has finally done me in, which sucks because I really didn't want to die anytime soon. Anyway, I decided to make this tape so I could say a few things that I've wanted to say to certain people just in case I didn't get a chance to say it to them when I was alive.

So let me start with my good friend Jim. Jim, you taught me how to fly fish and you gave me your friendship and I will never forget that. I hope that you tell a few stories later tonight about some of our times out on the Big Blackfoot. We had some great times drinkin' and fishin' and just talkin' and I cherished all of them. I love you man."

"I love you too John." Jim yells out.

"Next, I want to say to my new step-daughter Jessica, I'm glad that you told your mother that I was an alright guy and that she had your permission to date me. Your mother told me that if you did not approve that we would have never been together so thank you for that. I love you and do me a favor and take care of your mother for me. I worry all the time about what will happen when I am gone and I don't want her to be lonely or sad."

I look over and Jessica is attached to Sarah left arm, they are both smiling with tears in their eyes.

"Next, I want to say a few words to my son Andrew. Now I'm not sure if you are there right now, I'm about to head

down to Flagstaff to see if you want to drive back to Montana with me for the wedding. If you refused and you're not there then I told Sarah to get this tape to you somehow so you could see it. I hope you are there though and I hope we made that drive up and I hope we reconnected on some level."

I can feel Sarah's eyes on me as I watch.

"I hate how we lost touch son. It gnaws at my soul every day of my life. I miss you son, more than you could ever imagine and I want you to know that I love you. I also want you to know that even though your mother and I have passed on, I have left a loving family for you to be a part of. Everyone in that room is now your family and I want them to take care of you and I want you to take care of them. You are welcome in Montana whenever you want; our home is your home." Sarah looks at me, wraps her arm around mine, and squeezes.

"You are always welcome here." She says and I smile and squeeze her arm back.

"Next, I want to say a few words to my soon-to-be wife, Sarah, who I assume is my wife at this moment, I hope I made it to the wedding. Anyway, Sarah, my love, my rock, I love you so much. I'm sorry all of this went down like it did. I did plan on sticking around for years and years and years, but I guess the cosmos had other plans. I don't want to get into too much here. I could talk about you and us for hours, hell for days. What I want to say, besides how much I love you, is that I don't want you to give up. I know it sounds so cliché, like a line from a movie, but it's true. You will grieve and there will

be a healing period, but at some point I want you to move on and find another love. Don't give up. If I would have given up, I would have never found you. And I will be watching you so don't wait too long to get back on that horse. I love you babe, take care of yourself."

Sarah kisses her hand and blows it towards the television.

"Now for all of those that I didn't mention by name just know that I love all of you too and you all added to my happiness and I am glad that I got a chance to know all of you. Now, stop this tape, go toss my ashes into the Big Blackfoot, drink some beers, eat some meat, and have a great time. And don't forget to put on the CD I made just for this special occasion. I love all of you, now hit the stop button. Sarah, hit the stop button. Sarah, it's the big red button at the top, hit it now." My father winks and Sarah does as he says.

"Okay, everyone let's head down to the river and we will do as John says." Sarah instructs. Everyone gets up and heads out of the living room, out the back sliding glass doors and down towards the river. Jessica and I attempt to get up but Sarah pulls us back down. "Not so fast you two. I want you both to know that I've set aside some of John's ashes for both of you to do with what you want. I kept a tiny bit for myself too."

"Thank you." I say.

"Yeah, thanks mom." Jessica adds.

"Alright let's go do this."

The three of us stand up. Sarah grabs the box of ashes from

the fireplace mantle and then the three of us head out to join the others down on the bank of the Big Blackfoot. When we get down there Sarah opens the box and says a few words.

"John loved this river and now he will become a part of it, forever a part of it. And every time we look at it we will remember him and what a great man he was. We love you John." And with that Sarah pours my father's ashes, most of them anyway, into the Big Blackfoot. They disappeared immediately, dissolving into the waters of that mighty river, which had welcomed him for eternity. All I could think about at that moment was the fact that two days ago we were standing on this exact bank celebrating my father's wedding to Sarah and now she, his wife of only a few days, was pouring his ashes into the Big Blackfoot. The Big Blackfoot, the river he loved, the river that changed his life, the river that brought them together, the river that brought us together, hell, the river that brought all of us together.

We all made our way back to the house and did what my father had asked us to do, we partied. We drank several beers, we ate barbequed everything, and we told stories about our best times with my father, their friend, her love. We played the CD that my father had made and laughed at the music he had selected. The first track was *Stayin' Alive* by the Bee Gees. My father, the comedian. The rest was a collection of his favorite songs, everything from John Denver's *Leaving on a Jet Plane* to The Rolling Stone's *Gimme Shelter* and classics such as Elton John's *Benny and the Jets* and The Eagle's *Hotel*

California. It was a sad, happy, crazy, memorable night that no one that was there will ever forget. I passed out around two in the morning, I think, after quite possibly drinking a case of Moose Drool and way too much tequila.

CHAPTER TEN

I awake to the smell of something delicious permeating through the bedroom door. I lay in bed for a few minutes trying to figure out what and who is cooking in the kitchen. I come to the conclusion that it is Sarah and she is cooking pancakes and bacon. I sit up for a few more minutes, then get out of bed and throw on some pants. I exit the room and head to the kitchen. Sarah is standing with her back to me in front of the stove. I see a plate full of bacon next to her on the counter next to the stove.

"Good Morning." I say.

Sarah turns her head around and smiles. Her eyes are still a tad puffy. "Good Morning Andrew." She turns her focus back to what is on the stove. "I hope you're hungry."

"I am." I say even though I am not that hungry. My stomach is still loaded with beer and barbeque from last night.

"Good. I have some bacon here and I'm working on some chocolate chip flapjacks right now. There's a pot of coffee ready too."

I crack a smile. "You are amazing." I make my way over to the coffee maker.

"I don't know about that, but I can definitely cook a mean breakfast." She looks at me and smiles as I fill a coffee mug with caffeinated black gold and Irish crème creamer. "There's a couple plates and forks over there on the island."

"Okay." I take my coffee over to the island and set it down. I grab a plate and just as I do Sarah turns around with a fresh, steaming chocolate chip pancake on a spatula and sets it down on my empty plate.

"Help yourself to the bacon. I will have another flapjack ready in a couple of minutes."

"Okay. Thank you."

"You are very welcome." I walk over and add two strips of bacon to my plate. I make my way back to the island and sit down on one of the stools. I add butter and maple syrup to my hotcake. I cut into it with my fork and take a bite. The hot, chocolaty, buttery, maple flapjack melts in my mouth. It is almost too sweet so I take a bite of bacon to offset the sweetness. Then I take a drink of my coffee to offset the saltiness of the bacon. There is an exact science to eating, not only breakfast, but every meal.

"So when do you plan of heading back to L.A.?" Sarah asks as she sets a fresh flapjack on her plate.

"Well, I should get back as soon as possible. I need to get back to work so I can pay the rent." I take another bite of my pancake.

"How are you getting back?" I don't answer as I ponder the question and take a bite of bacon.

"That's a really good question, I haven't even thought about that." Sarah smiles and then leaves the kitchen. I take another drink of my coffee. She returns and sets an envelope and a key on the island next to me. "What's this?"

"That is an envelope and the key is to your father's truck, which is now your truck." She smiles and then heads back to the stove to make some more flapjacks.

"Really? Are you sure?"

"Of course. I don't need it and he would want you to have it anyway."

I take the key in my hand and look at it. "Okay. And the envelope?" I set the key down and grab the envelope, which has my name written on it.

She turns and looks at me. "I have no idea. Your father told me to give it to you when…" She pauses as tears well up in her eyes but she battles them away. "…Well you know." Sarah turns back to the stove as I carefully open the envelope and take out the single paper that is inside. The paper is a check in the amount of ten thousand dollars.

"Holy shit." Sarah turns and sets another flapjack on her plate, looks at me, and smiles like she knows about it. "I can't take this."

"I don't know what you're talking about, but whatever it is he wanted you to have it so it's yours." She winks at me and smiles again.

"Wow, this is too much. I can't even fathom this right now." Sarah turns to make another flapjack.

"Well, just put it back in the envelope and deal with it later. It's not going anywhere." I do as she says. The insanity of the past week and a half is making my head feel like a fucking pinball machine during a multi-ball round. I finish my first hotcake and right on cue, with her back to me, Sarah says, "Have another flapjack." I take one off of her plate and place it on mine. I add butter and maple syrup to it and kill it in under a minute. I finish off my second strip of bacon and then wash it all down with the rest of my coffee.

"Well, I guess I'm gonna leave today if that's okay. I mean if you're okay. I don't want to leave you here all alone." She turns and adds a final pancake to her plate. She smiles at me.

"I'll be fine Andrew. I have Jessica and my folks and friends here, but I do want you to promise me something."

"Anything."

"I want you to promise me that you'll come up here and visit us at least once a year."

I smile at her. "I promise." She smiles. "And you're always welcome in L.A. if you ever want to explore the city or spend some time at the beach."

"That would be fun. Jessica and I just might take you up on that."

"I hope so. I would love to have you guys down."

I stand up and take my plate, fork, and coffee mug to the sink. I rinse everything off and out and place it in dishwasher. Then I give Sarah a hug and then I head to the bedroom. I shower, get dressed, and then pack. Jessica comes over to say goodbye and the three of us chat for a bit about my father and about visiting L.A. in the near future.

At noon, I throw my pack onto the passenger seat and close the door. I give Sara and Jessica hugs goodbye and then I hop in the driver's seat and start up the truck. I take the tiny urn that contains a small amount of my father's ashes and place it on the dash. I wave goodbye, put the truck in gear, and head out onto highway 200. I reach Interstate 90 and jump on the on-ramp headed east towards Butte.

The plan, which I devised while I was in the shower, is to stop in Salt Lake City for the night. Then, instead of going through Vegas and straight to Venice, I'm going to check out the Grand Canyon since I've never seen it. Then I figure since I'm close I might as well go to Flagstaff and see Raelynn before I head back home. Of course with my luck she won't be working, but I figure I will just leave it up to fate.

Just before I reach Butte I jump on Interstate 15 and head south towards Salt Lake City, which I reach at eight o'clock sharp. I grab a spicy chicken sandwich meal at a nearby

Wendy's and then I check-in to a cheap motel for the night.

The next morning at seven I skip breakfast and jump back on Interstate 15 and continue south. Three hours later I head east on highway 20 for a short distance and then I jump on highway 89 and head south through southern Utah. Ten minutes later I reach the small town of Panguitch and stop to get something to eat. I find a Subway sandwich shop and grab a foot long B.L.T. to go. I eat half of it as I continue south on highway 89.

An hour later the highway splits at the tiny town of Kanab. I stop and get some gas and then jump on highway 89A east just north of the Grand Canyon. Almost two hours later I meet back up with highway 89 and take it south through the northern Arizona nothingness. I eat the other half of my B.L.T. and wash it down with a bottle of water I bought when I got gas in Kanab. About an hour later I take a right and head west on highway 64 southeast of the Grand Canyon. A little over an hour later I reach the south rim.

I head down the park entrance road, pass the visitors center, and park in the parking lot at Mather Point. I get out and as I walk towards the canyon I am in awe. The enormity of this canyon is indescribable. When Max and Bear told me about it last year they tried to describe it but couldn't really. They said it was unreal, like an enormous painting, and I now understood what they meant. It is truly grand, no pun intended, but that's really the only way to describe it. It is aptly named and for good reason. Just looking at the depth of the canyon and seeing the millions of years of erosion takes you back in time to when people didn't even exist. I wish I had time to hike down to the Colorado River like they did, but I don't, I need to get to Flagstaff tonight.

After a few more minutes of awe-inspired sightseeing I head out of the park and head south on highway 64, which is also highway 180. Thirty minutes later the highways split, the 64 goes straight south to Interstate 40 and the 180, which I take, heads south east to Flagstaff. I reach Flagstaff and the Denny's an hour later. It is now almost six o'clock at night and I am certain Raelynn isn't working since she served us breakfast last time. I was correct, but was told that she works in the morning. I grab some food anyway, a Cheeseburger and fries and then decide to check-in to a cheap motel. I fall asleep while watching a House Hunters marathon on HGTV.

I wake up to the alarm on my cellphone at eight in the morning. I shower, get dressed, and then check-out of the motel. Then I head to Denny's to see Raelynn. When I get there she is not there yet and so I just take a seat on one of the stools at the counter. I order coffee, but wait to order food until she arrives, which she does thirty minutes later. She looks flustered, but smiles when she sees me.

"Hey you, did you come back to see me?" I nod my head.

"I told you I would."

"Ah, you are too sweet. It's Drew right?"

"Yep, you remembered."

"I did."

"So where's your section?" I ask so I can have her serve me.

"Right here. I'm a tad late so another waitress is covering my tables and now I get the counter."

"Well I guess I'll just stay here then."

"Have you ordered food yet?"

"Nope, I was waitin' for you." She smiles that big beautiful southern smile, her green eyes glow like jade.

"You know what you want?"

"Yes ma'am, I will have two eggs scrambled, hash browns, a side of bacon, a side of grits, and an English muffin."

"Okay, I will get that goin' and I'll be right back with some more coffee for ya."

"I would appreciate it Raelynn, thank you."

She walks over to the kitchen and I watch her the whole way. Her curvy figure and great ass gives me the chills and I smile. She returns with a pot of coffee and fills my mug.

"Thank you."

"You are very welcome. Let me check on this other customer and I will be right back."

"Okay." I grab a couple packets of sugar, tear them open and add them to my coffee. I also add some creamer and stir it all together. I take a drink as Raelynn appears again. "So why were you late this morning?"

"Ugh, car trouble."

"Oh yeah, what happened? Flat tire?"

"No, I'm not sure, it just died on me. I had it towed to an

auto shop. They are supposed to call me when they find out what's wrong with it."

"Well hopefully it's nothing too serious."

"Yeah, let's hope so, it's not like I have a ton of money and I don't budget for this sort of thing."

"I hear ya."

"So where's your dad?"

I take a few seconds to answer. "He actually passed away a few days ago."

Her eyes get wide and her jaw drops open. "Oh my God. I'm so sorry."

"It's okay, you didn't know. He had cancer and didn't have long. We thought he had a little longer, but that's how it goes sometimes."

"I can't believe it, you two were just in here less than two weeks ago."

"Yeah I know, but he made it to the wedding."

"The wedding?" she inquires.

"Yeah, the day after we were here we headed up to Montana and he got married and then he didn't wake up the next morning."

"Oh my God, that is the saddest thing I've ever heard."

"It was sad, but it was amazing too. The entire trip was so unbelievably amazing. I can't even tell you how much it meant to both of us."

"Well, that's good."

"Yeah."

"So where are you headed now?"

"Back home."

"And where is home?"

"Los Angeles, well Venice to be exact."

"Like Venice Beach?"

"Yeah, same thing. Have you been there?"

"No, but I've heard of it, it's a pretty famous place."

"Yeah, I guess it is."

"I think your food is ready, let me go check."

"Okay."

She walks to the kitchen and returns with my breakfast. As soon as she sets it down her cellphone rings. She grabs it and answers it.

"Hello…Are you serious?…Well shit, what am I supposed to do now?…Okay, well let me figure out what to do and I'll call ya back in a bit…Okay, bye." She hits the end call button on her cellphone and puts it back in her pocket.

"Bad news I take it?" I inquire. She looks at me with a cute little frown.

"I apparently blew my engine. It's dead, my car is dead."

"Damn, that sucks."

She stands there and I can tell she is in deep thought as to what to do. She snaps out of it. "I'm sorry, I just totally spaced out."

"It's fine."

"You know what? It is fine. It's just a damn car. I mean you just lost your father, there is no way I'm gonna cry about a car."

I crack a smile. "Yeah, but you need a car, it's important." At that moment I have a crazy, but totally sane idea. I pull the key to my father's truck out of my pocket and set it on the counter in front of her. "Here." She looks at the key and then at me.

"Here what?"

"Take it, it's yours."

"What?"

"My dad's truck, I want you to have it."

Her green eyes get as big as beach balls. "No way, I can't accept that."

"You can and you will."

"No way."

"Look, Raelynn, I just got it two days ago and I don't really need it. I was just gonna drive it home and then sell it anyway."

"You already have a car at home?"

"Nah, I don't have a car, I hate driving in L.A. traffic. I don't really need a car, I just walk or bike it."

"I can't just take this, it was your fathers."

"Yes it was and if he was here right now he would give it to you too. Just take it. I want you to have it."

"Well let me at least give you some money for it."

"Not a chance."

"Well, I don't know what to say?"

"You don't have to say anything."

"Well thank you." I smile and she smiles back at me.

"I'm gonna at least buy your breakfast."

"Okay, I'll let you do that."

"And I want a hug." I laugh.

"Okay." She comes out from behind the counter and gives me a big southern hug. She smells like bacon and floral perfume and I am in heaven. We end our embrace and stare at each other. My heart is racing.

"Can I call you sometime?" I ask.

"Of course you can."

She gives me a kiss on the cheek and I blush. I sit back down and finish my breakfast while she grabs a pen and writes her number down on a clean napkin. I get the number, she pays my bill, and then we head to the truck so I can grab my pack out of it.

"Wait a minute, how are you gonna get back to L.A.?"

"I'll just jump on the next Greyhound Bus out of town."

"No way. Let me drive you?"

"No, that is way too far and you have work. I can take the bus, it's no big deal."

She looks at me for a few seconds not sure what to say. "Can I at least take you to the bus station?"

"I don't know can you?"

"Yeah, someone will cover for me. It's not that far away."

"Okay."

She runs inside and comes out a couple minutes later with her purse. She drives me to the Greyhound Bus stop. I get out and grab my pack. She gets out and walks around the truck. "I can't believe this day so far, this is crazy."

"Me either, but it's been great. I'm glad I can help you out."

With that she plants a huge kiss on my lips and it is electric. After that I kiss her again and it is ever better. "You better call me." She says with a smile.

"I'll call you tonight."

To that she smiles that huge southern Georgia peach smile and I head to the bus stop to buy a ticket home. She hops in the truck and takes off back to work. I purchase a one-way ticket for ninety bucks. The bus will be here in two hours so I wait. When the bus arrives I jump on it and eleven hours later I get off at the Los Angeles Greyhound station near downtown. I grab and taxi, which costs me forty-five bucks and takes twenty-five minutes.

When I finally get home I head straight to my bedroom and toss my pack on the floor in front of my bed. I head to Bear's room and knock on his bedroom door. There is no answer so I open it and peek inside. He is not there so I head to the kitchen to grab a beer. I notice a note on the refrigerator held there with a magnet we got from a local pizza joint. The note reads:

WENT TO MAINE TO CLIMB KATAHDIN.
MIGHT VENTURE INTO CANADA.
BE BACK IN A FEW WEEKS.

DON'T EAT MY FUCKIN' LUCKY CHARMS.

BEAR

I shake my head as I grab a beer from the fridge. I open it and take a swig. I read the note again, shake my head again, and say, out loud, "that crazy bastard."

I love you and miss you dad.

(T.A. Maxwell Sr. 1954-2012)

T.A. Maxwell was born in Southern California.
He is the father of one son and one daughter.
His current whereabouts are unknown.
This is his third novel.

Also by T.A. Maxwell

The Zen Lunatics
I Am Joe American and Other Poems
Broken Like Vinyl
Into The Ocean
Sexy, Smart, Crazy Beautiful

The Following Pages Contain a Sneak Peak
of T.A. Maxwell's Prequel to On The Road To Big Blackfoot:

The Zen Lunatics

"I want to see the Space Needle," I announce out of the blue as I lie sprawled out on the living room couch in my blue plaid boxer shorts, shirtless. Empty beer cans, wine bottles, an ashtray full of cigarette butts, and a six inch clear plastic bong litter the top of the used coffee table I picked up at a local Goodwill last summer.

"Okay," says my friend and roommate Drew, who is lying on the love seat in his favorite pair of Superman tighty-whitey underwear, also shirtless. He is a recent convert to the Zen lunacy that is our way of life. And by our, I mean myself and our other roommate and friend Barry, who is only called that by his family, we call him Bear. He is sitting in the comfy, puffy green chair in his tie-dyed robe, which he stole from a not-so-classy hotel in Santa Barbara a few months back and which he tie-dyed himself. He, of course, is wearing nothing underneath and is half asleep. We are all hung over, watching an episode of House Hunters International on HGTV.

"Well?" I say.

"Well what?" asks Drew.

"I want to see the Space Needle."

"Well get on the computer, find a picture of it, and look at it."

"No man, I want to see it in person."

"It's in Seattle dipshit," adds Bear, who I thought was asleep, but apparently he was just resting his eyes or possibly in deep meditation.

"No shit, I know where the Space Needle is."

"We are in Los Angeles. Seattle is like a thousand miles away."

"It's actually more like twelve hundred miles Drewski. We could be there by this time tomorrow, come on guys."

"You're fucking crazy Max, why the hell would we spend all that money on gas and food and lodging to look at a structure we can see on the internet?"

"Because a picture is shit man, it's nothing. Seeing it in person is spiritual, it's like real live crazy meditation, you can't get that from a picture. We can even go to the top of it and look out and see Puget Sound and Mount Rainier, and fucking Canada man."

"You're crazy man, but what the hell, let's do it, Bear you

down?"

"You know I'm down. I love Zen lunatic road trips. Especially to the great northwest," Bear's eyes are still closed and he is quite possibly still in some sort of meditative state.

"Fuckin' A, lets pack," I yell.

We each pack a bag, which include the essentials; clothes, a toothbrush, and deodorant. I pack the toothpaste. Drew packs the protection, for possible violent and/or sexual interactions. And Bear packs the weed. It is late April and the weather is great in L.A, but I suggest we each bring a light jacket just in case. The weather in the great northwest can still be a little chilly this time of year. After a couple of hits on a small joint and a quick snack, which is just a bowl of Lucky Charms, we head to the car, our packs in hand. It is almost noon on a Monday. We jump on Interstate 405 and head north, Bear is in the backseat, Drew is in the front passenger seat, and I am behind the wheel of my black 1996 Jeep Cherokee.

"I might get fired for this Max," Drew says with a slightly concerned look on his face.

"Nah, just call in sick, tell them you got that flu bug that's been going around."

"I don't know man, I told them two weeks ago I had the worst case of Hershey squirts in recorded history and I don't think they bought that shit. The next day at work my boss just looked at me and shook his head like he knew I was bullshittin'."

Drew works at a small popular grocery chain in West Los Angeles. Bear used to work there too, that's where they met. I knew Drew from high school and met Bear through him.

Drew's boss is a dick, a total douchebag. He spends his entire shift hitting on the female workers and yelling at the male workers, trying to impress those chicks with his authority and shit. He thinks he is so fucking cool, but he's not, he's a fucking manager at a grocery store, there is nothing cool about that.

"Fuck him man, he can suck my dick," Bear chimes in from the backseat. The guy fired him for opening boxes of food and eating it on the job, so he is not a fan of his.

"Yeah fuck him, I'll write you a legit doctor's note and it will be all good man," I add.

"Yeah fuck that motherfucker," Drew yells as he cranks up the stereo, which is playing Lynyrd Skynyrd's *Sweet Home Alabama*. We all sing along, even Bear, whose eyes are still closed, possibly still meditating, as we head north on Interstate 5 through the Grapevine.

I don't have to worry about being fired, because I don't have a job. Well that's not true, I'm a writer, but don't tell my father that's a job, at least not a real job. "Anyone can write boy", he would say to me every time he asked me what I was doing for work and I told him I was writing. I would always reply with "yes they can father, but that doesn't mean they can write well."

My relationship with my father is somewhat complicated. He left when I was eight and disappeared for fourteen years. Then one day, out of the blue, he called me. I was a week away from graduating from college and he wanted to come and watch me walk across the stage since he missed it when I graduated from high school. Why? I still don't know, but I told him he could do whatever he wanted, I just didn't want to talk to him before or after. He agreed and when the day came all I could do was search for him in the crowd.

I don't even remember the speeches or even walking across the stage, all I remember was looking, searching for my father in the stands, not even knowing who I was looking for. I never saw him, at least I don't think I did. A couple of weeks later he called again and I agreed to meet him for breakfast.

The meeting was mostly just us eating with a little conversation in between the chewing, all of it initiated by him. He apologized for leaving and not keeping in touch, but said that he started a new family and was busy with that. All I said was that it was okay and that I had gotten over it the night of my graduation after hours of thought, along with some beer and weed. I left out the latter. He was glad and said he wanted to see me again. I said that would be cool and six years later we still keep in touch, mostly through phone calls and text messages. I have flown to Sioux Falls, South Dakota to see him and my step-mother and my half-brother and half-sister a few times. They are a nice bunch and I am glad that we could all reconnect and put the past behind us.

"What are you thinking about Max? Or are you in that wide-eyed Zen meditative state you like to be in?" asks Drew.

"Just thinkin' Drew boy."

"And what are you thinking about Maximilian?"

"Oh just thinkin' about how drunk we're all gonna be tonight."

"Hells yeah Maximum overdrive."

"Did someone say drunk?" Bear interjects, his eyes finally

open, wide, wider, widest, with his head coming towards me, smiling, and finally kissing me on the cheek. We all bust out laughing as we merge onto northbound Highway 99 and head into Bakersfield.

We stop at a local gas station in Bakersfield for some gas and snacks. Drew grabs the usual; some beef jerky and a couple energy drinks. Bear always gets a green tea and a bag of Funyuns. He thinks he is such a Zen lunatic because he drinks green tea. I always give him shit because Snapple green tea isn't fucking Zen, its corporate bullshit, the complete opposite of Zen. I grab a coffee, fair trade from some South American country of course, and an apple fritter.

After we gas up and grab our goodies, we continue north on Highway 99 instead of Interstate 5 because, well, Interstate 5 up through central California is a goddamn bore-fest, just cow farms and rolling hills. At least on Highway 99 you drive through several towns on your way up to Sacramento, which passes the time a lot quicker. Just north of Bakersfield I see a hitchhiker.

"Let's pick him up."

"Who?" asks Drew as he looks around.

"That hitchhiker." I point at a guy walking north on the right side of the highway as we pass him.

"No way man. You know you're not supposed to pick up hitchers man."

I pull over on the gravel shoulder about a hundred yards ahead of the hitchhiker.

"Dude, this is not a car full of chicks. We are three men, he's not going to fuck with us," I explain as I extend my left arm out the window and wave him to come on. I look back and he is jogging towards the Jeep, almost there.

"Besides, we could use the road karma."

"Road karma?" asks Drew.

"So we don't blow a tire man or die in an accident," Bear chimes in.

The hitcher jogs up to the front passenger window.

"Hop on in man," I say, shooting my thumb towards the backseat as Bear, without direction, scoots over and sits behind me.

"Thanks man," the hitcher says as he opens the rear passenger door and climbs in.

The guy I am guessing is around our age, mid to late twenties, but he looks older because of all the dirt on his face and clothes. It's not like he's covered in dirt, but you can tell that he has been on the road for a while. He is wearing a pair of tan chino pants and a blue and green plaid cowboy type shirt. He is also wearing a navy blue bandana that is keeping his dirty blond dreadlocks from attacking everyone in the vehicle. He has a moustache, one of those handlebar jobs but it's scraggly and could use some wax. His pack is an old army pack that he probably got at an army surplus store somewhere.

"Thanks again man, I really appreciate it."

"No problem. Where you headed?" I say.

"San Fran."

"Alright, well we are headed to Sacramento so let's see how close we can get you." I grab the road atlas I have had for years and start thumbing through it.

"So what's your name fellow traveler?" Bear questions.

"Well my given name is Joe, but my friends all call me Crazy J."

I turn my head away from the map and look at Drew whose eyes are as wide as the Grand Canyon staring right at me and non-verbally telling me, I told you so.

"Why do they call you that?" I inquire.

"Well, the crazy part is because I'm always doing crazy shit like those Jackass guys. You know jumping off of shit, skateboarding naked, shit like that. And the letter J is cause my name is Joe, so..."

Drew's eyes relax and I go back to examining the map.

"So what's your guy's names?"

"Drew. Introductions please," I say still trying to figure out the best place to drop Crazy J off.

"Okay. Well I'm Drew." He points at himself. "That's Bear." He points at Bear. "And this is Max." He points at me and I give our new temporary companion the thumbs up.

"Nice to meet you guys."

"Alright Crazy J, it looks like Manteca is the best we can do. From there you just have to hitch a ride straight west and you should be in Frisco in no time."

"How far to Manteca?" Drew asks.

"Looks like about a three hour drive, two and a half if I get a little heavy on the pedal."

"Sounds perfect man, you guys are lifesavers."

"So, you smoke, Crazy J?" Bear asks as he opens his eyes.

"Smoke what?"

Bear's eyes open wide and then wider as he slowly leans in towards Crazy J and says in a Vincent Price voice

"Weeeeeeeeeed."

"Yeah man, why?" Crazy J says slightly terrified. Drew and I try hard not to bust out laughing.

"Cause if you didn't, we were gonna have to kill you and turn your skull into a bong." Bear could not keep it up and started laughing before he could even get the word bong out of his mouth. Drew and I follow and all three of us laugh uncontrollably for a good three minutes. Crazy J didn't know what to think of the scene. I thought for sure he would jump out and take off back towards Bakersfield running hysterically, but he didn't. He went from slightly terrified to super terrified to laughing with us.

"Bet you didn't think you were going to catch a ride with a bunch of Zen lunatics when you woke up this morning did you?" I say while smiling at him through the rearview mirror.

"Sure didn't."

"I think you need a little wacky weed my brotha," Bear says to Crazy J.

"I think we all need a little of that my brotha," I add.

"I second that," chimes in Drew.

"I third that," proclaims Bear.

"Well, roll that shit up and let's get our asses on the road," I say as I put the Jeep into drive and merge back onto northbound Highway 99 kicking up gravel and a cloud of dust in the process.

We make a quick pit stop in Visalia to use the bathroom. By now we have a good little buzz going from the joint we shared, so Crazy J runs in to grab some munchies as the rest of us load back into my Jeep.

"We should take off and leave him," says Bear.

"What the hell for?" I say.

Bear, now in the front passenger seat leans towards me and whispers "because he's a fucking hippie and I hate fucking hippies."

I lean in towards him, our noses almost touching and whisper back "dude, you are one more tie-dyed shirt away from being his brother, brother." I smile and give him a little head butt.

"Fuck you man, he stinks, fucking patchouli and B.O., its killin' me."

"We should fuck with him," Drew interjects.

I turn my head towards the backseat and say "what's on your mind Drew screw?"

"How about when he gets in the car I will say that we are out of smokes and I need to run in and grab a carton. I will pay for them but I will run out of store like I stole them and then we take off."

"I like it, let's do it," I reply.

Just as I say this Crazy J exits the store, walks to the Jeep, opens the rear passenger door, and climbs in. Right when he shuts the door the plan goes into effect.

"Shit man, we're out of smokes. I'm gonna run in real quick and grab a carton for the road."

"Yeah, you better, we're gonna need some smokes," I say.

Drew exits the car from the left side, jogs around the front of the Jeep and enters the store. Not thirty seconds later he bursts out of the store holding a carton of smokes, sprinting towards us. He violently opens the right rear passenger door.

"Scoot over man, quick, quick, quick," Drew yells, breathing heavily. Crazy J quickly scoots over with a confused look on his face. Drew slams the door.

"Go, go, go," Drew yells.

I had already started the Jeep when he went into the store, so I put it in drive and peeled out, ass hot, out of the parking lot and got back onto Highway 99 heading north.

"What the fuck Drew? Tell me you didn't do a grab and run?" I yell.

"Hells yeah I did Maxi man," Drew smiles and then looks at Crazy J, serious face style and says "You don't have any warrants, do you?"

Crazy J, still in shock, takes a few seconds to respond. "Warrants? No man no warrants, but shit man I don't want to go to jail."

Bear looks out the back window, "Shit man is that a highway patrol cruiser back there?"

Drew and Crazy J turn quickly and look out the back window. I look at the rearview mirror and by God if there wasn't a highway patrol car three cars back in the other lane. This prank could not have gone any better up to this point. Hell, even I had forgotten that this was a joke and thought to myself shit we are fucked, which I repeated out loud.

"Shit, we are fucked."

Bear added "fuck man, I still have a shit ton of weeeeeed on meeeee." At that I started to think that I should probably drive the speed limit, because even though the cigarette theft was a joke, Bear did have a shit ton of weed on him and I was still a little high. We did not need to be stopped by no hi-po.

By this time, Crazy J was shitting his pants, probably literally, the guy did stink.

"Hey, you guys need to look forward, if you're all looking at him he is gonna know something is up," I say. They all turn back and face front. I look at the rearview mirror and notice that Drew looks a little nervous, too nervous.

"Drew, you alright?"

"You gotta get off this highway man, like now," he says. He is starting to sweat and freak me out.

"And why do I need to do that? You did pay for the smokes right?" Crazy J looks at Drew and then back at me trying to figure out what is going on.

"Yeah, I just didn't pay for this Zippo lighter." Drew holds up a shiny silver Zippo lighter. Crazy J is beginning to realize what is going on.

Bear jumps in "You dumb bastard, you know we have weed in here, fuck."

I take the next exit, just north of downtown Selma, and the highway patrol car exits right behind us.

"Cop's exiting too, he is fucking right behind us, shit." I say. Crazy J turns and looks out the back window.

I yell "Dude, what the fuck are you doing, face front, face front." I take a right fully expecting to see blue and red lights behind me. No lights. I pull into a Burger King parking lot. No lights. The highway patrol car continues down the road. We are safe, for now. I pull into a space and turn the Jeep off. I turn towards Drew.

"Dude, what is wrong with you? All you had to do was buy a carton of smokes, run out of the store, and jump in, simple, easy, and you had to make it an actual theft." Drew's frowny face transforms into a dipshit smiley face and he starts laughing uncontrollably. The three of us all look at each other like, what the fuck is so funny?

Drew laughing says "The Zippo is mine. I didn't steal it, I've had it for years."

"You motherfucker," yells Bear. I look at Bear and shake my head "this fucking guy," pointing my thumb at Drew. Bear and I start to laugh and as we laugh it continues to get louder. Crazy J is fucking lost.

"So did you steal the lighter?" he asks.

"No," replies Drew, still laughing.

"What about the carton of smokes?"

"Nope." We are all laughing harder now.

Crazy J is pissed and he grabs his pack from the back "you guys are fucking crazy man, I'm outta here, thanks for the ride." He exits the Jeep, slams the door, and heads into the Burger King.

"Bear, I think Drew is now officially, a Zen Lunatic."

"Yep, this crazy motherfucker got us good, a fuckin' prank within a prank, classic."

"Should we go in and apologize to Crazy J?" I ask.

"Nah, fuck him, he doesn't even deserve to be called crazy, he should change his name to Stinky J," Drew says and we all laugh.

"Shit, we should start calling you Crazy D," Bear added.

"Alright, fuck him, we gotta get to Chico by night fall anyway, let's get back on the road."

I start the Jeep, put it in reverse, and back out of the

parking space.

"Chico? We stoppin' for the night?" asked Drew.

"What. I didn't tell you guys?

"Noooooo," Bear answers.

"I thought we were driving straight through to Seattle?"
Drew added.

"Well, I thought we would all enjoy a little pit stop in
Chico for the night so I called a college buddy of mine and
asked if we could crash out and maybe hit up the bars tonight.
He said it was cool, so it's on like Donkey Kong."

"It's Monday night man, are the bars even open in Chico?"
Drew asks.

"I take it, Drewski that you have never been to Chico?"

"Nope"

"Well, I went to college there and I assure you the bars are
open. The fucking college has always been rated a top party
school and shit, all students do there is party. Hell, there was
even a riot back in the 80's that shut down the town's Pioneer
Days celebration forever. The bars are open bro."

"Well shit, lets rock n' roll," Drew yells.

Bear adds, "Step on it Max, I wanna see some titties."

I enter the on-ramp and we continue north on Highway 99
all the way to Chico. The four hour drive to Chico went by
real quick. We jammed out to various songs on various radio
stations, snacked on junk food, and threw back several energy
drinks that made us fly high. We sang every song that came on
the radio, if we did not know the words we made up our own
or tried to guess what the singer was going to say. We did not
do much talking, but we laughed every once in a while as we

thought about Crazy J and the double prank that made him bolt, poor bastard.